AF449447

LIFE'S TUITION FEES

Author: Alex Tsotros
Title: Life's Tuition Fees
Text translator / editor: Sevi Tsiligroudi
Cover designer: Roza Papoutsaki-Rapti

Production supervisor: Platon Malliagkas
www.mediterrabooks.com

ISBN 978-618-00-3358-8

Alex Tsotros

Life's Tuition Fees

A Diamond Dealer's Baptism by Fire
in South Africa

ଈଔ

To my grandson
Alex Guilloteau

Preface

Looking back, I'm thinking about how this book has reached the shelves of stores and how it got on Amazon as an ebook. This has nothing to do with selfishness or personal gain, but merely my core desire to help my good friend Frank come out of his isolation by telling his story to the world. The stigma of falling for his best friend's con will stick with him for the rest of his life. Those that have suffered at the hands of conmen know this stigma well. The readers, I believe, will understand both my words and the powers that pushed me to write this story.

There have been, and will be, thousands of similar cases of honest people that fall victim to scammers. Some victims are tormented with

shame, pervasive anger and thoughts of ven-
geance. I think it is time to break the silence,
gather stories and opinions so we can empower
people to deal with such crises before vengeful
thoughts reach maturity. These tactics

remind me of today's "Me Too" movement.
I am therefore triggering the alarm to invite
everyone - colleagues or otherwise - who have
themselves been victims of financial fraud, or
know about similar cases, to come forward in
solidarity. Gathering all this information in a
blog will pass on our experience as a legacy to
young people with the ultimate goal of avoiding
and punishing fraudsters.

Introduction

I haven't slept in the last few days. Not only do I get no sleep whatsoever, but the nights are nightmarishly dark, the kind that makes you believe you're going crazy.

What I have experienced in recent days is beyond imagination, something no one would ever conceive, not even as the most unimaginable nonsense, or the deadliest black humour.

Nothing in this story adds up or can be interpreted by the human mind or square logic, although one can often find excuses or rational explanations. Nevertheless, there is no logical explanation for someone stabbing you in the back in such a horrible, devious manner. What's more, being screwed by someone who's been

your best friend and partner for years, your ide-
alised role model, the hardworking, rich guy, the
owner of import and export companies - not to
mention a leasing company, recently upgraded
to a bank by the Reserve Bank of South Africa
-, a well-known dealer of rough and polished
diamonds, a big stock exchange player... Well,
it's a bit like Bill Gates coming to steal your loaf
of bread.

When you cannot fall asleep at night, as we
all know, the mind struggles to find answers
to every single one of your recent worries and
misadventures. On the edge of its logical limit,
it starts jumping to quick, convenient rational-
isations that seem to make sense. On the third
sleepless night, my mind returned to what is
called "Once upon a time ..."

From the first conversations I had with Mr.
Karantoglou, my "friend" in question, I told
him:

"Remember, my friend: We have started a
partnership and a good friendship. Don't try to
screw me because I will respond in such a way
that you will not be able to tell the difference

between your head and your ass."

And we both laughed.

But the time has come. There is nothing else left but revenge! To make myself clear, it's not revenge, but rather punishment, the hardest possible punishment one can get. Real punishment! The next moment, as I was tossing and turning in bed, I touched the handle of the revolver I keep under my pillow: a special .45 that a friend of mine, a German gunsmith, had custom-made for me, with bullets that could kill a bull.

We are still friends and business partners with Karantoglou, so he doesn't know what's coming his way. This suits me just fine because it makes my decision easy to make. I have been working on my plan for the last couple of nights: it is easy, no one will see me, and he is not going to understand a thing, not until the long barrel of the revolver he carries reaches his mouth.

It is seven in the morning, and I'm driving toward Karantoglou's office. It's time to meet him, as he is disarming the alarm at the back entrance of his office. I follow him upstairs to the office. In ten minutes, it will all be over and then by ten o'clock, I will be on my appointment with Louis in Pretoria.

I don't know if anyone can imagine the pleasure I am experiencing. It feels like I'm about to eat a lobster spaghetti dinner in ten minutes, washed down with a glass of French cognac.

I can still remember the frame on the wall of my parents' house, back at my home island:

Το πεπρωμένον φυγείν αδύνατον
(Destiny is unavoidable)

But let's start from the beginning. My name is Frangiskos Hasides. My Portuguese friends in South Africa used to call me Franco and, later on, my Jewish friends called me Frank.

Chapter 1

The morning of July 1st, 1971, was a hot one in Athens, and I was ready to fly to South Africa. A few months before, around Christmas, my wife and I had decided to leave Greece. After five or more years in the Greek Public Service (The Agricultural Bank) for me and seven years in the Ministry of Education for my wife, with countless irrational incidents with daily interventions from third parties and senior executives, the decision was made. If we were to stay in Greece, we would be consumed by stress way before retirement. Stress, but without benefits, that is. Stress for... doing our job correctly... that was our constant reward.

It was irrational or funny, or whatever you

prefer to call it. On one day, I was taking an oath in the "Gospel and the Pope" to abide by the laws and regulations of the bank, and on the next day, senior executives and politicians were asking me to break that oath, exerting tremendous pressure to approve loans for their own friends, contrary to the laws and regulations of the institution. My personal tactic, and the proper approach toward the service, was "If you are eligible for a loan, you will get it, regardless of any objections from above - always for political reasons," which often attracted reactions, sometimes so stupid that everyone laughed. Suffice to say, there was one incident at the Agricultural Bank when I sent a geotechnical study to the branch manager. Ten days later, a letter came from the headquarters in Athens accusing me of "ignoring the bank's fundamental regulations" and asking me to provide a formal apology. What constituted "ignorance of the regulations"? I had signed my letter to the branch manager with "Yours sincerely," unaware of the law of 1923, according to which I should have signed with "Yours respectfully." In this way, I had offended the branch manager - a horrible mistake!

Then, my friend, there was the military junta that ruled in Greece from 1967 to 1974. State executives were forced to make speeches on the enormous benefits the regime had brought to the country. So I found myself on the squares of several villages talking about the junta. I remember one such on-demand speech I gave at the theatre of Atalanti. When I finished, the redneck chief constable came to me and said, "Well done. You said it right, but you should have shouted a little more."

So, I decided to shout a little more, spit, and then shit on everything. Eventually I managed, not without effort, to take a six-month unpaid leave and fly to South Africa. My wife was to join me a little later. It was my first long-haul flight, and so it was something new for me. I will never forget the experience, or rather the feeling and the impressive state of mind I found myself in when we landed at Johannesburg International Airport. It was the feeling of warmth that I always felt when I went back to the island where I was born and raised. It was the feeling of returning to the place where you were born, to your homeland. The warmth and the comfort someone yearns to feel on each arrival. I accepted this as proof that my choice to visit and live in this place was correct (after, of course, meeting with the state's competent authorities and obtaining permission to live and work permanently in the country).

In six months, I got the residence permit, and we had to decide what to do to start making money. The approach and the conduct of the authorities of this country were indeed impressive. From the very first moment, they treated us as serious people who could be helpful to them once we had proven our abilities. When all put together, my wife and I had six hundred dollars. Neither exercising my profession as an agriculturist nor starting my own farm was wise. The Agricultural Bank of South Africa had farms to dispense to capable farmers free of charge, provided that the beneficiary would stay there permanently. This choice would be an instant failure for me due to several problems: different climate, the people's mentality, various working languages and dialects... not to mention the wildlife.

Then, the opportunity to work in the Cape area came up, specifically in Stellenbosch. You see, I specialised in viticulture and winemaking, and the people in charge would be happy to hire me, knowing Greece's level in this field. But I thought that if I were to become an employee, I could have stayed back in my country, where my monthly income was around twelve thousand drachmas, quite an amount at a time when the salary of a teacher was about two thousand drachmas.

My city, the one I eventually chose to live and work in, was Boksburg East, close to Jan Smuts Airport, Johannesburg, and all the malls, shops, and businesses. Pretoria, the capital, where all of the government services, foreign embassies, and central banks were located, was no more than 50 km away via the highway.

The solution I found to make a living was to open a "cafe,"[1] a mini neighbourhood mar-

____

1 Cafe: Pronounced cáfe, it is the trademark shop of South Africa, the equivalent of the Mini-Market of Europe and Greece.

ket that also sold cigarettes. Having a cafe was a profitable job because it was not easy to find a vacant space to open such a shop, especially if another one was located nearby. You see, in this country, there was an Urban Planning Authority, which means that one could not start a business anywhere he pleased outside the locations designated by the state authority. Essentially, the cafe was pretty much a monopolistic operation.

Another reason for my choice was that I could secure direct funding from one of the two tobacco wholesalers. The owner, whom I only met once, was one of the smartest business men around, and known to me only as the "Cigarette Guy". The Cigarette Guy knew the exact value of each shop back to the time of the company's existance. Small or large, he could unmistakably calculate the turnover from the sale of cigarettes, and of course, the profits. Think about the daily revenue from selling cigarettes to a population of forty to fifty million. Even if only half of them smoke, you can understand that his turnover was higher than that of the largest bank in South Africa. The idea was this: The Cigarette Guy financed anyone who wanted to buy or open a cafe, with the provision that the store would exclusively sell the cigarettes and whatever other stuff he would provide, such as candy, chocolates, and smoker's accessories.

"Outspan Cafe" was the name of a small shop that was on the verge of bankruptcy. I agreed upon the final price for the purchase, not with the current Afrikaner owner, but with the one who had sold it to him, i.e. the previous owner, who was a real estate broker. The reason was that after three or four months of holding the store, the Afrikaner had used the money from the sale of the original stock to purchase a new Jaguar instead of buying much-needed supplies. What an opportunity for me! I closed the deal – of course after coming to an agreement with the Cigarette Guy – at seventeen-thousand dollars. The Cigarette Guy handed me five-thousand dollars: two thousand for the deposit and another three to stock up. He would also give me credit for five-thousand in supplies until I would have turned over this amount, after which time

I would start reimbursing him without interest. The remaining value of the shop was arranged in monthly instalments of five-hundred dollars, payable to the initial owner. Then the bank approved an open loan of two-thousand dollars for me. In six months, my turnover had increased enough to pay the expenses and leave me with a profit of around two-thousand dollars.

Before leaving Greece, I had started taking evening courses at the Higher Commercial School, known today as the Athens University of Economics and Business. I dropped out in the second year because of my move to South Africa, but what I had already learned proved useful throughout my life. I still remember the professor telling us in every class:

"Always remember the equation:

labour + capital = financial result. If there is not enough capital, you will have to put in more personal work to achieve a better outcome until your capital has grown enough to buy labour too."

This equation has always been with me in whatever I do, and it always works.

The second thing I had to do was buy a weapon, a handgun – a vital tool. To obtain a gun permit from the police, you had to present two witnesses who would guarantee that they knew you and that you were a good and peaceful citizen. At least one of them had to be an Afrikaner. Within a month in the store, I became acquainted with several clients, including a Police Detective who was the son of a frequent customer. He guaranteed it for us. Then I went to Benoni, the nearest town, where there was a hardware store, and I bought my first weapon, a thirty-two inch pistol with a double safety click and an eight-round magazine. I chose this one because it was easy to wear on the belt or underarm without being noticed.

After about five months, the Afrikaner who was holding the instalment bills for the shop (around thirteen thousand dollars due) came in, and he said:

"Franco, I have decided to sell your promissory notes, and since you are the one directly interested, if you want, think about it today and make me an offer."

Now, what does it mean to sell promissory notes? You have the so-called "discounters", who buy promissory notes, bank checks and loans, for almost half the price. This way, the seller receives money instantly, depending on the loan's repayment rate or the signatory's obligations. So, I went to my bank, the Standard Bank, told the story to the manager and asked him if he could help me. He looked at the file and replied that it would depend on the amount. I asked him how much money he could help me with, and he said, "I will give you seven-thousand dollars for twenty-four months. Make an offer to the owner of the notes and, if he accepts, come with him at the end of banking hours, around four in the afternoon, to close it."

After accepting the offer, almost half of what I owed him, the owner and I went to the bank together. The director himself wrote the agreement, examined the notes for their authenticity, and gave the owner a check for seven thousand dollars. All this was done simply and quickly - the manager saw a hardworking customer and, therefore, a lasting relationship that corresponded to profits for the bank - without any commission whatsoever!

My second business I started myself. One of Outspan Cafe's first customers was Nick Meyer, a tall Afrikaner former police officer who had left the force to start his own real estate business and was currently building new stores nearby. Due to the excellent relationship I had with him and his wife, who was also a customer of Outspan Cafe, he gave me the largest of all his shops, where I started a Cafe-Delicatessen called "Tivoli".

When the Cigarette Guy found out about my new store – after I had paid off my previous debt – he came to meet me himself (a great honour for me) and said, "I will send you a designer for your store, and I will furnish it for you. In addition, you will have ten-thousand dollars in merchandise and cigarettes. You will repay them all in twenty-four instalments without interest."

Tivoli became a remarkable store from the outset, with clients from the City Hall, the courts, and lawyers. This was because, in addition to the usual snacks, I started baking pastitsio, pies, and various other Greek delicacies, and also offered a wide variety of books and magazines, fine cheeses, and cold cuts.

During my tenure in Tivoli, I had the opportunity to meet many Greek and foreign businessmen, including Mr. Karantoglou, a guy taken straight out of 1930s New York, what with his hat and English jacket. You would always find him at auctions of storage rooms and dry cleaners. Rumour had it that he was selling expensive dry cleaning machines in instalments and then put them up for auction again if the buyer fell behind two or three consecutive payments. There was something Greek-Turkish about his demeanour and his appearance as a formidable trader, which was reminiscent of old merchants from Smyrna.

When the time came to sell Tivoli – and this is important – I had already found another store right across the street from Tivoli, from the same constructor, Nick Meyer. It is a big deal to know someone like Nick Meyer. (I remember that his wife loved Greece and Greek women. She always said she liked the fact that Greek women never smoked on the street. You should see what's happening nowadays, Mrs. Meyer).

Looking for businesses other than catering and cafe-related ventures, I thought that venturing into the dry-cleaning business was not a bad idea. As I was looking for laundry and dry cleaning machines, guess who I stumbled upon: Mr. Karantoglou. Our first professional contact ran with polite, friendly conversations about our current businesses, past jobs, and so on. On the other hand, I learned that in addition to trade agencies, he also owned a leasing company shared with his father, one that I had heard of, the Alfa Leasing Co. I remember the morning when I first went into his office, crossing a sizable room that looked like an exhibition hall full of machinery, until I reached the mezzanine where his office was. As I stepped in, the phone rang. He apologised to me, turned to the handset, and started giving instructions to buy and sell stocks in the stock exchange. Similar calls followed regarding diamonds. I was impressed by all this.

The truth is that he had an outstanding engineer who taught me the first secrets of the profession. Davides, as the Greeks used to call David Zelman, was a well-educated Jewish guy who knew machines like the back of his hand. This turned out to be really significant for me because he tried to convey everything necessary for the laundry business when he realised I was receptive to learning. Of course, we also talked about Karantoglou. He described him as an excellent professional who had a lot on his mind aside from machinery; essentially stocks, diamonds, a leasing company, and much more.

This way, I started my first dry cleaning business, BETA Dry Cleaners, in Boksburg, Transvaal. In addition, I also opened a Laundromat with coin-operated machines right across the dry-cleaner. On the advice of David Zelman, the first machine I bought was a second-hand one that used alkaline as a detergent. This was the most expensive and the best kind of kerosene, which performed better at lower temperatures than PERK, the detergent that was widely used, which, as I used to say, boiled the clothes. You could clean all the delicates, even suede or leather. I soon got the hang of it and became a laundry expert. Of course, not everyone could operate such a machine, and most importantly, you could not leave it with anyone from the un-skilled staff. The latter was a common practice in this industry, especially to the Greeks, who used to have someone unqualified do all the work.

Laundry and dry clean owners nearby were dropping by to see what was going on, always worried that their own business would be im-pacted. Upon seeing a small dry cleaning ma-chine, they calmed down. Because the device was relatively small and, in fact, not even new, word came out quickly that "Franco has bought a bucket to kick us all out of business."

One of the first customers to bring clothes for dry cleaning, who later became frequent, was a customs officer, an old acquaintance from Tivoli. Amazed to see me at BETA Dry Clean-ers, he said, "Franco, are you the owner here?"

"Yes."

"But, what do you know about laundry? Until yesterday you were baking pastitsio and pies."

"My grandpa was a legendary dry cleaner! And I always wanted to follow in his footsteps."

"Then prove that it's true. You must prove yourself, my friend!"

"Rest assured that I will."

The dry cleaning business, later enhanced with clothing repair, was doing very well, and it was time to buy a second machine. You see, the use of alkaline not only cleansed but rejuvenated fabrics, but the machine was expensive and complicated to operate and I had to operate it myself. Soon, all the employees and pilots of South African Airways and other airliners were bringing in their uniforms and clothes for cleaning. In less than twelve months, always having the equation in mind and putting in a lot of personal work, "BETA Dry Cleaners" gained the people's trust and expanded into five branches, four of which also rendered clothing-repair services. Of course, there was also the laundromat next to the main store, with four washers and dryers.

In twenty-two months, a potential buyer came up and offered me $120,000 in cash, so obviously, I sold it to him. It was Mr. Van Halen, a wealthy guy who had severe problems with the tax office. It was great luck that the business was exactly what they needed to launder not only clothes but also money. I was the businessman of the month for my bank. I also paid off Karantoglou, with whom I had already started a very close and sound commercial relationship.

After successfully selling the dry-cleaning chain, the first thing I thought of was taking a short vacation, which would combine rest and preparations for my next entrepreneurial step. Early on, as far back as a year before I sold the business, I had developed an interest in buying diamonds. When Karantoglou heard of this, he started talking about his own business as a large-scale trader of diamonds. To show me how large his stock was, he said, "If I put all of my diamonds into a single row, they will reach Durban (a city 600 kilometers away)."

He also confided that when grading diamonds, some of them, while low in quality, were nice in appearance and had a particular snow-like beauty. There are typically called frosted. So, he gave me some of them as a consignment (also commonly known as "On Appro," from the English word "Approval"). He explained to me that in the diamond trade, trust between the merchants - whether big or small - was imperative because it was impossible for someone who had a potential buyer to prepay the supplier since the sale is usually far from certain. Customers, with few exceptions, rarely buy at first glance.

"Well, I trust you with these diamonds on Appro, and we'll see how it goes," he told me.

Thus began the next stage of my relationship with Mr. Karantoglou, since I was out of work and I had his assurance for stock supply on consignment.

I was straightforward with him back then.

"You know, Dem (this is what I used to call him), a lot is being said about you in the business world, so I want to make something clear from the beginning. Do not fuck me! I will counter with the mightiest blow! You have to keep this in mind throughout our friendship and our cooperation."

He started laughing.

"We may fuck everyone, but never each other, Frank!"

In the meantime, I enrolled as a correspon-
dent student in the Gemological Institute of
America (GIA) and the Jewellery Council of
South Africa's. It was a good move towards entering a broader circle of diamond dealers, as
they called us - an easy way to get inside the
business.

Chapter 2

Later on, the idea came up to move into a new house with more amenities since we had already received an excellent offer to sell our own. Looking for a new residence is an enjoyable activity, particularly in South Africa, where you could find many properties suitable for all tastes. I was opting for a large plot with a spacious house and a swimming pool, not too far from my workplace and the region we were all used to.

Eventually, after many visits to numerous houses and with the help of a very experienced lady from a renowned real estate agency, we found our home, in a good location and with many advantages. Within walking distance from the city centre, in a plot of three thousand square metres, with its own water supply and an Olympic-sized swimming pool. It was funny how we got it. Apparently, the lady from the real estate office got tired of us and said, "Let me show you a fantastic house, so if you like it, I will know precisely what you are looking for."

We crossed a beautiful garden and knocked on the front door of the house. A gentleman came out, whom our estate agent seemed to know.

"Can we take a look at your place?" she asked him. "This family is looking for a house, and I wanted to show them yours as an example."

"Well, you can take a look, he said, but this house is not for sale."

A moment later, as I was stepping out on the backyard, a vast, park-like space with a huge pool where a girl was swimming, a lady came out of a room and asked. "What do these people want?"

"They are looking for a house," her husband replied, "and I am telling them that this one is not for sale."

"Hold on, why not? Let's talk about it," said the wife.

This was followed by a dispute between the spouses, eventually won by the wife, and the bargaining began.

"How much do you offer?"

From then on, everything was clear and the house was ours.

Before leaving the laundry to the new owners (you see, it takes a month of adjusting and monitoring the work for the new owners plus one permanent employee to get acquainted with the job and the clients), I started looking for a new office or shop/office where I would commence my diamond business, my newly chosen profession. I finally found a space in a small arcade in Boksburg, in a good commercial location, on the ground floor, a short walk from a street with plenty of parking.

I remember a large supermarket nearby where, every day, I used to see two young girls creating transparent sculptural figures for its advertisements. I asked them if they had some spare time to make a sculpture for my shop's window, a scale model of the Kimberley diamond mine, better known as the "Big Hole." Indeed, two days later, the "Big Hole" was on my window sill, so I put some diamond-like crystals in it, and it became something extraordinary. "Kimberley Diamonds" was the name of this new business venture. "Good luck," I wished myself.

Next door was another empty office. I rented this under my wife's name and made it a shop with ballet accessories because a relative of Dave's had the dealership of these monopolistic items, which would secure enough customers. For me, it was a solution because, when I was away for work, someone had to be in my office or at least nearby, mainly to answer the phone since customers always made appointments before coming.

Being used to opening supermarkets or delis, I began to advertise the opening of the office in the surrounding towns. On opening day, having the diamonds Karantoglou had given me on Appro, I made a buffet of snacks and wine in anticipation of the coming customers. The first week passed, the second came, and then the third... and nothing. I started having doubts about this job and did not believe it could exist as a viable business. This is the difference for someone who switches from a deli owner to a diamond trader. In supermarkets, work commences on the first morning that the store opens because customers want cigarettes, bread, milk, and the store starts counting dollars one by one.

A fellow dealer by the name of Dinos, a Greek who was selling diamonds for a small African company, happened to be passing by my office and thought we should meet. He asked me if I needed any diamonds and showed me one good quality, yellow stone, 1.6 carats. With his consent, I immediately started advertising it in a weekly magazine, the Farmers Weekly, read almost all over Africa. Since then, I remained in contact with Dinos, exchanging information and generally helping one another. The retail price of this diamond was around $9,000. I could have it for $4,500, and I was advertising it at $6,000. Two days after the publication of the magazine, Nicolas Lombard, a farmer who lived six hundred kilometres away, called me and said, "I'm interested in this diamond if you still have it."

I immediately called Dinos, who assured me that he had it and gave me the address to find him, if my customer would finally come. I replied "yes" to the customer, who came the next day in his old Jeep, in which we then drove to Dino's apartment since he did not have an office of his own. The customer saw the diamond and bought it immediately. It was my first closed deal, and that was when I realised that with diamonds, you do not make a daily turnover of one hundred dollars, which will eventually give you a monthly profit of around two to three thousand. Two or three deals per year will leave you with the same profits.

A little more of the courage I needed after my prolonged inactivity was given by a neighbour, who came one afternoon to welcome us to the neighbourhood. When he asked about my profession and I answered "diamond dealer," he was excited.

"Fantastic! When people discover you, you

will be doing an outstanding job before you know it because, as I understand, you are solemn and honest."

I will mention another incident, my second good deal, not only in terms of money but also in terms of, as they say, expanding the customer base. You see, I started on the first of December, and when the holidays came, I sold some small diamonds and I made new acquaintances; not only customers but also diamond dealers, a key element for finding merchandise and benchmarking the prices Karantoglou was giving me, with whom I was doing very well, since on the one hand I was selling and on the other, he could see that I was honest and plain dealing.

So I started advertising in the local newspapers throughout Boksburg and Germiston – there were two main ones; the STAR and the Pretoria News. It was Christmas Eve when a potential customer called and told me in an earnest tone that he really wanted to buy one diamond and possibly one ring I was advertising. Still, he could not come to my office because he had a problem with his legs and begged me to go to his house myself.

It was nothing new. I often visited houses in the city and even remote farms to show the trade and close a deal, since it was common to receive house calls for advertisements. It goes without saying that not all callers were really interested in buying, especially some old ladies who often wanted to just take a look at some beautiful gems. The difference here was that the address I was given was behind Hillbrow, in a location, if not dangerous, then at least suspicious, so I asked a friend of mine to come along. When we arrived, at around nine in the evening, I asked him to wait in my car and instructed him to go to the police if I wasn't back in thirty to forty minutes. I was also carrying my gun, of course, but in such cases, what matters is who pulls first.

It turned out to be the family of a well-off gentleman whose leg was injured and he could not walk. He owned a coal mine and had an affinity for gems. In the adjacent apartment lived a few painters who used to buy diamonds! Suffice to say, I sold two diamonds and exchanged another two for paintings. This deal was exciting because, among other things, I met this family of painters, who for many years were supplying me with art at low prices, which I then sold, for cash or for diamonds, to Jewish dealers interested in art.

In the meantime, after the tools and instruments I had ordered from the Gemological Institute of America had arrived, the office had turned into a small lab, where I studied, practised, and kept trying to comprehend the precious stones.

It is worth making a parenthesis here because many do not know, and they believe that diamond carats are related to gold carats. The gold carat is a degree of purity, with 24 carats corresponding to 100%, while in precious stones, the carat is a unit of weight. One carat of the gemstone is equivalent to one-fifth of a gram; i.e. 5 carats is equal to one gram. The carat is then divided into 100 points (we write half-carat as 0.50ct, 10% of a carat 0,10ct and so on). If you ask how the name "carat" came up, there is some interesting history behind it.

In ancient times, there were no electronic or mechanical precision scales but the so-called balances. You'd put the stone or whatever else you wanted to weigh on one saucer, a counter-weight on the other, and calculate the weight accordingly. Middle Eastern traders in those times used carob seeds as counterweights be-cause they are hard, almost unbreakable, and, when ripe, they always weigh the same. In fact, I have tried it myself many times: five seeds weigh one gram. In the Oriental languages, car-obs are called "haroop" or "caroop," which has come to our days as carat, or "ct" for short.

It should also be noted that the prices of di-amonds of the same weight differ and adapt to their different categories. The value of a dia-mond depends on four factors; the 4 Cs. First of all, the carat weight: the larger the diamond, the higher the value. The second factor deter-mining the price of a diamond is the colour (in fact, not actual colour, but a tint, scaling from yellow to colourless). The first well-known dia-monds in South Africa were yellowish and were usually found along the banks of the Orange

River in the province of Cape Town. The more colourless a diamond is, the higher its value gets because absolutely colourless diamonds are rare. In South Africa, we still use the names given by the first miners: Blue-white (today's D), Ice White (E), Fine White (F), Top White (G), White (H), Top Commercial White (I), Commercial White (J), Top Silver (K), Silver (L), and the Cape family from L and below, ranging from yellowish to yellow. Third is clarity, which is related to crystalline excellence. Most crystals bear signs of imperfection or external wear, and when examined under a microscope, they present internal defects in the crystal formation or external fractures. The purer the diamond is, the higher its value rises. The current clarity grading in descending order is FL, IF, VVS1, VVS2, VS1, VS2, SI1, SI2, I1, I2, I3. Finally, you have the cut. When talking about diamonds and their prices, we always refer to polished stones. The cut will eventually show the full beauty of the crystal. It can be round, square, marquise, oval, pear-shaped, etc., and the finer it is, the higher the value of the diamond. So, when one hears "1.27ct, H colour, SI1 clarity, brilliant round cut", then one has all the criteria required to evaluate the stone. Of course, such information must be provided by a certified expert on diamonds and their properties.

The impact of my advertisements in the newspapers was highly enhanced by a 1.27-carat diamond, one of the "frosted" Karantoglou had given me, which became a great success. It was round-cut, the lowest grade of clarity, ice white colour, without much sheen, and the selling price was 10% that of a similar good-quality diamond. I was advertising a 1.27-carat diamond for $250! Private buyers and many professionals, impressed by its low price, came to see this diamond, which I was guaranteeing for its weight and natural origin, but not for its quality. Those who knew about diamonds were asking me if I had anything better. I always did, and always at very low prices, close to the actual wholesale price. You see, I was opting for a mere 10-15% profit instead of the 100-150% made by other dealers, and I was offering the assurance that the quality of the four essential attributes (the four Cs) was solid. So in two or three months, after the New Year, my customers were not only private buyers but also specialised dealers, particularly from Pretoria.

The first diamond dealer to visit me after reading about the "1.27 carats" in the Pretoria Newspaper was Louis van der Berg, a young, educated accountant with practical knowledge of pedology. He had many prominent customers, especially Afrikaner farm owners from the countryside, who were known for their money as well as their undeclared income. Many of them even owned private planes. Louis van der Berg became my best customer because I was giving him the lowest prices. He, in turn, had many resellers touring the country, and those had many farm owners as customers, with money that they invested in diamonds.

The relationship with Karantoglou, on the other hand, had reached a certain level of friendliness on both ends. In fact, our families had begun to meet up, especially for Sunday barbecues, either at my house or his, which was closer to Johannesburg, half the distance than from mine. I had quickly become his best customer or, better yet, his best salesman, as I was selling more and more diamonds, always on Appro, and I was one-hundred percent punctual on my payments. Suffice to say that my turnover from diamond sales had reached a value of over two to three-hundred thousand dollars per month. He would often invite me to his house to have some whiskey and discuss diamonds, finance, and future plans to develop our relationship and cooperation.

A peculiarity of the lives of diamond dealers is the way they get to know each other. You go to someone's office, you start a conversation, another dealer comes in, he joins the discussion, introductions follow, and the critical question pops up: "Do you work for a firm, or do you run your own business?" When the answer is "I run my own," there is a lot of interest because you are a potential customer for every dealer. This is because no diamond factory or sales office has, nor can it have, all diamond categories and sizes in stock. This is particularly true in South Africa, where diamonds are an indispensable part of the peoples' identity due to their history and the fact that they are found in almost every square acre of the country.

A serious diamond dealer must have a sound reputation of being honest and an expert in their field, i.e. diamonds and jewellery. At the beginning of his career, he usually sells diamonds from factories and big dealers, depending on his reputation, which, after all, quickly becomes known. In the long run, saving money, he slowly builds his own stock, buying from anywhere he can find reasonable prices, usually from the factories he already cooperates with. His course depends on his personal quality and his sound knowledge of diamonds, not only in theory but also in practice. Let's not forget that the grading and value of each diamond are not written on it. Anyone, dealer or factory owner, can make a mistake, because while they might know the cost of buying the rough diamond, they don't know the actual value of the finished product, from which they expect to make a profit, something that is quite uncertain.

Merchants source diamonds from factories in

two ways. The first one is to opt for specific categories, for example, "I want four diamonds, 1.10 to 1.20 carats, I-J colour and VS clarity." Then the merchandise comes complete with certificates and the price goes up. Otherwise, they buy from the stock when the factory has completed polishing a set of gems. In such cases, they go to the boss, who tells them: "Pick what you want, and I will tell you the cost." The dealer takes a look, makes two or three piles of stones (he may have made three batches of the same category), asks for their price, and waits. The boss starts: "This lot costs so much, this one so much," and the dealer decides what is best for him. Usually, when the dealer is new and spends a lot of time looking at a stone, the boss reckons that he likes it and is eager to have it, and – guess what – the price goes up. In short, they are both playing a shell game, and the best man wins. Be that as it may, when going for quantity, you are never sure how good your purchase is because of the speed with which the deal is made. So when you get back to your office, you start to carefully examine all the stones to determine whether or

not this was a good deal. The diamond whole-
saler always has this buying stress. Whatever
happens, one thing is certain: Good deal, good
luck. Bad deal, bad luck, with no returns. After
a good purchase, you can afford to sell to other
dealers, jewellery stores, and private buyers.

There is a standard process in the diamond
retail market, mainly involving young couples
who intend to get engaged. An engagement
will only happen after the groom has presented a solitaire ring, with the diamond and the
design of the girl's choice. Therefore, a professional diamond dealer's role is not just to sell
the diamond but often to create the jewel. Having foreseen this demand for jewellery design, I
took jewellery design courses in addition to my
studies at the GIA.

That January morning was pleasantly cool and
sunny. As usual, I was sitting at my desk reading
the Pretoria News when the first phone call of
the day came in.

"How can I help you?" I asked.

"I'm interested in the diamond you are

advertising in Pretoria News, the 1.27 carat. Is it available?"

"Yes, if you want, you can come by. It's easy to find me."

I gave him the address and asked for his name.

"I am also a diamond dealer, and my name is Jacobus Snyman."

An hour or so later, a well-shaped gentleman came to my office, who explained that he worked for ESKOM, the South African electricity company and that he was involved in the diamond business in his spare time.

"I will be able to buy diamonds from time to time, but I prefer to know your stock or anything else you have that I can sell."

His manner was typical, and after discussing things for a long time, mainly for me to decide what kind of person he was, he invited me to his house in Pretoria. I am saying all this to conclude that Jacobus Snyman became one of my best clients and a dear friend for many years. His clients were usually government officials, civil servants, and many farmers. Together we managed to reach a yearly turnover of around twenty-thousand dollars.

In less than an hour after Jacobus had left, I received another exciting phone call, this time from a Jewish diamond dealer. It was the "Giant," and I am saying Giant because he was so enormous that he could not find clothes in his size to wear and was always in sportswear. His name was not Goliath but David, Dave for short, Bernstein. I had recently met him through Harry Levine, a Jewish associate and now friend, a jewellery specialist with whom I cooperated in serving my retail customers – who were increasing day by day thanks to the "1.27 carat" that attracted them. I must note that my acquaintance with Harry was a remarkable conjunction because he was a good man, a good craftsman, owned a perfect workshop of ten craftsmen, and implemented any design he was given in a short time. He, too, was introduced to me by Karantoglou, who was also giving him his own business.

When I first met the Giant, he told me that he was a salesman for the Berkowitz Diamond

Company (the brother, as I later found out, of the well-known bankruptcy lawyer) and was willing to give me diamonds on consignment. He was a pleasant, witty, short-fused guy, and we quickly got to know each other better. He asked me to call him, and I soon made a habit out of calling him every morning at his office and, if he was still there, going to have a cup of coffee, smoke a Marlboro cigarette, and of course, discuss work. The second time I went to his office it was very early in the morning, and as I was sitting facing the door, something behind it caught my eye. Curious, I approached and read:

"*Do not forget the school fees.*"

"What is this? I asked him."

"It's something that I should always remember as a hefty debt. It reminds me of the cost of school fees I have paid to be here and my duty to pay back one day."

And he went on to explain, "Frank, I used to have my own office, my own stock, perhaps not very big, but big enough to make a great living. I don't know how long you have been in the diamond industry or if you have heard of the scandal involving Venter, the 'king' of sports cars. This guy was wealthy; he owned the largest and most powerful financial company in Pretoria, collected sports cars, and changed wives every year to get the latest 'Miss' of anything he could touch. And, apparently, he was a keen collector of many expensive diamonds. His latest acquisition was the Public Bank, a small bank based in Durban.

I was lucky to get hold of a diamond he was looking for, eight to ten carats, G or F colour, VVSi clarity, whose value at the time was around $70,000. You can understand the profit I made, even though I sold it to him for a price very close to the wholesale price. Satisfied as he was, he bought another stone, making me really happy. The first time he paid me in cash and then by check from his bank. His last order was a carved ring with a matching necklace and earrings, all together for $200,000. When I returned to my office, I was so excited that I immediately called my friends and girlfriend to tell them everything. My luck flew away the next day when I went to my bank to cash the check. The teller looked at me closely, asked me to give him a minute (not a second, as they usually say) and left to go find the manager, with whom he returned to make my day: 'The Public Bank, Dave, has its doors closed. You'd better read the news. Mr. Venter, the owner, has too many liabilities, and the bank does not have enough money to back him. Go try, if possible, to get your jewellery back.'

On my way back to the office, I was about to go crazy with this bad news. That fucking bastard Venter was buying diamonds and cars with the money he took from people of all social levels. The latest story was that when the financial police broke into his house in Pretoria's Waterkloof Park, they found five Lamborghinis, five Aston Martins, five Porsches, and five brand new Ferraris in his five-hundred square metre garage. Most of them had been bought with money from his bank, money deposited by private investors, who for many months had been "receiving a monthly interest" of 12% from their deposits, and brought in their friends and associates to invest their money too and make even more."

In fact, the plan was not really new, rather quite old: You give me ten thousand dollars, and I will pay you 12% interest on your money every month. How can I do this? The first month is easy, but I will probably pay you with your own money in the second.

An investment with such a big return is news that travels fast. You talk to your relatives, your friends, and, above all, to yourself: "For such a profit, let me take all the money I have saved and invest it." I know some wealthy Greeks who trusted him with a lot of money just to make his life easier. He was taking money from one person's deposits, to pay interest to someone else, and so on. Now, what happens if someone asks for a full refund and another does the same, and so on... Kaboom! Cannon!

Dave continued, "The misfortune, my friend, was that I gave him the jewellery at the last and worst moment. Had it been one day later, I might have saved my ass. All this is a lot for school fees, my friend. I had to pay with my own flesh and blood. Besides losing all my capital, I also had to reimburse my boss, whose diamonds had been nabbed by the bastard. The note behind the door is to remind me of the "school fees," namely all the money I have lost and the importance of having my eyes open at all times."

It was the first time I learned the famous term "school fees." The money I've lost to scammers.

Chapter 3

One good thing about my acquaintance with Dave was that I met several diamond dealers both small and large because in addition to knowing your realm, gaining the experience of buying and selling and learning the tricks of the trade was imperative. Having started alone and without any real friends, I had to build relationships with as many diverse "types" in the game as possible.

Eliot Prischman was a remarkable dealer, despite his young age, with a fairly large stock of diamonds apparently inherited from his mother's family. He had helped me many times, especially with big stones, the women's favourites for exceptional jewellery, but medium in terms of price and quality. I met him one of the many times I was having coffee at Dave's office. Eliot was not exactly a dealer with profound knowledge, but he knew enough to look at a stone and roughly estimate its quality and wholesale price. He was also good at bargaining, the game of "how much do you offer? No, that's too little, give me a little more. Well, yes, but it is not quite as you say…" In short, he was good at the shell game. When you got to know him well, you realised that he was a good family man and an honest dealer.

That day I heard from Dave that a new, large diamond-cutting factory was about to open and he would probably start working there. He told me that he knew one of the three partners very well.

The factory was called Candor. One partner was Trevor Katz, the South African General Manager. He used to also have a famous clothing factory he later sold. The second partner, Eliot Moshe, was the CEO, a wealthy guy from Israel. And Maes-Debois from Belgium, the 'big gun' in the sales of primarily large stones.

Dave was certain he was going to get a job at the factory as a sales manager. This would be very good for him, and me too, since I would be able to access "difficult" stones, the industry's most common problem. When he finally got the job, I was the first to hurry to his new office to congratulate him. Happy as he was, he said, "Have a seat. I'll buy you coffee if you spare me a cigarette."

"Well, this is awkward because I've quit smoking. Done. Finished!"

"Fantastic! I've been meaning to ask you to."

We had just started drinking our coffee when someone walked in who I thought was the big boss. Dave introduced me.

"Mr. Trevor, meet my good friend and customer, Mr. Frank."

Trevor gave me the impression of a pleasant yet blunt type. I attributed the latter to the fact that we didn't know each other well yet, and, in diamonds, everyone is being assessed for their potential as a client and their honesty, or lack thereof. He struck me as a good and kind man, so I told him a few things about myself and how I ended up becoming a diamond dealer. I also informed him about my previous activities, mainly to show him that he was not the only one who had been in many different businesses.

"Dave, I don't think I am wrong. I like your friend and will like him more if he makes us money."

"Have no doubts about that, Mr. Trevor," I replied.

I had made a habit out of visiting Dave in his factory office after my early-morning visits to Karantoglou. Trevor had quickly become my friend, so I could have on consignment any diamond I wanted from the factory, and this way, I was able to source the scarcest stone a buyer could ask for. You see, it was at a time without fax machines and cell phones, so the information would travel by word of mouth. Therefore, knowing who had this or that diamond and where they had them was a massive advantage for a dealer, especially if they supplied other dealers. After all, by then, I had proved to everyone that their money was safe. Many Jewish dealers used to say, "Frank's word is as good as a contract."

The next day was Saturday, so for the fun of it, I asked Trevor and Dave to go out on Saturday night, at the opening of "Athens by Night", a club in Hillbrow. The name says it all. It was a Greek place with bouzouki, breaking plates and all, which was very popular, especially with the Jewish community, so everyone accepted the proposal with great pleasure.

On Saturday morning, Trevor called to tell me that his other partner, Eliot Moshe, had arrived from Israel and asked if he could come too. "With pleasure," I replied. Without exaggeration, it was the most enjoyable and fun night I had in ages. We danced, broke plates, ate meze, and, most importantly, got to know each other better. It was also an opportunity for our wives to meet, which was essential for enhancing our relations.

On Monday, Trevor was all smiles and thanked everyone not only for having a great time but also for having the opportunity to please the "Big Boss," Moshe, who had come with his girlfriend, so everyone was happy.

Chapter 4

The day had started well. First, Louis had found two more dealers in the province, one better than the other, connected with many farm owners. Johan Strydom and Andries Vender were to become Louis's big guns and an excellent sales channel for me. Second, my first ever customer turned up again.

That same night, Karantoglou invited me to his house for whiskey and future planning. You see, our commercial relationship was growing along with our friendly one. Visits to each other's houses were frequent and very enjoyable for the whole family, especially whenever he was in the mood for conversation and whiskey. That night, however, was all about our business relationship.

"Frank," he told me, "you have reached a high level. I am saying this because you are one of the best diamond dealers I've ever met, and I am guessing your profits should be proportionate."

The latter struck me as a sort of trap. It seemed to me as if he was expecting me to tell him how much I was making. Obviously, I'd rather die before telling anyone that my current earnings were around thirty to fifty thousand dollars per month. Karantoglou continued:

"On the other hand, I must also keep my boxes open and support you with a stock of around $300,000 since your business is going so well. Fortunately, your customers have turned out to be very good; their checks always clear."

Before giving diamonds to his people, Louis always asked for a deposit check, which he gave back if the diamonds were returned. I used to do something similar with Karantoglou, as he had asked me a few months before, "Frank, it's not that I don't trust you, but I need to have something too, for the IRS at least, because sometimes they come to check the stock."

So I used to write him a check for fifty

thousand dollars, which he returned to me when I gave him either checks or cash from my customers.

Karantoglou continued, "Listen, Frank. Why do things like children, with you giving me the check, me giving the check back... You should give me six checks of fifty thousand dollars, each one dated the first of each month starting from the following month and onwards. Two or three days prior to each due date, I will be giving you an equal check to put in your bank, and your own will be repaid. Now, on another topic, because many times you need me very early in the morning – I know you are an early bird just as I am. I think I have told you about the back door to my office: Instead of opening the front door in the morning to pass through all the machines and the security guard, I prefer to park in the back alley, which is always quiet, and use the small back door to the office. The doorbell is in the corner, behind the front gate. You'd better use this entrance too in the morning."

This suited me because I was often carrying a lot of cash.

"Good to know," I replied.

I had nothing to lose from this modification because I always had a corresponding stock of diamonds from him, so there was no problem. Work was always going well and fast, especially now, with Trevor and his factory. On the other hand, Louis paid in cash for the most part, and the amount he paid with his customers' checks was always low. The same applied for the rest of the buyers, mainly from Pretoria, but from other areas too, such as Springs.

Our meetings with Karantoglou grew more frequent, and our business still grew better. More family visits were paid to each other's houses, now with the presence of his father and mother.

Chapter 5

A week later, as I stepped into Karantoglou's office for our usual morning meeting, I found him really excited.

"Frank," he told me, "today's news is good. It is not that yesterday's was bad, but diamonds are a vivid business, and each day can be different to the next. Do you remember I had told you that I worked with the Seckell family factory to process the rough diamonds I had sponsored for them at the last Sight?"

At this point, I have to explain the meaning of the word "Sight": It comes from the De Beers Group, which, as almost everyone knows, at least until the early 90s, was the only authorised supplier of rough diamonds to processing factories all over the world. De Beers kept those factories tied with contracts that defined the monthly number of stones they had to buy. Customers that purchased from De Beers were known as Sightholders. De Beers would hold sales events, known as Sights. Around the first week of each month, the Sightholders went to the company's headquarters in Kimberley, where they received a "box" full of rough stones worth between 800.000-1.200.000 South African Rand, all without having the right to select or check the quality. More often than not, these factories did not have the financial capacity to process the contents, so they would try to find a sponsor or often sell the entire package to another dealer or factory. As many professionals in the industry were saying, the profit margin De Beers allowed to the cutting factories was minimal, and the slightest error in the processing of an expensive diamond would take that away. You see, the diamond's selling price does not depend on the cost of the manufacturer, but is based on the 4Cs I have mentioned before.

This means that a mistake in the processing of the diamond could cost the manufacturer a lot.

One well-paid profession in the business is the diamond architect, who will study the rough stone and outline the cutting and subsequent polishing process with permanent ink. Rough diamonds come in various shapes in nature (ball round, flattened oval, double cone, flattened cuboids, double but inclined cone, etc.), and apart from its shape, more often than not the stone has external or internal defects that will reduce the finished product's value if not removed. So, the architect's intervention is always necessary, particularly for the largest and most expensive stones. The owners of cutting factories always use such an expert when processing diamonds of high value.

To understand the significance of all this, I must also mention the case of a rough diamond, top D colour, weighing 9.78 carats. The seller was trying to persuade buyers that this could yield a processed diamond of 5 carats, top D colour, and flawless, nothing less than VVSi. There was a dispute around the final result, whether it would yield the 5 carats or the best clarity. Eventually, the buyer paid thirty thousand dollars. After cutting and polishing were nearly finished, with an arduous effort to keep it to 5 carats and as clear as possible, the final diamond came to 4.86 carats, D colour and VSi quality instead of VVSi. What does this mean in terms of money? A 5ct, D, VVSi diamond has an index price of $65,000 retail and $40,000 wholesale, while the corresponding values for the 4.86ct, D, VSi are $37,000 and $22,000, respectively. As a result, the factory lost all the purchase and cutting cost, plus another ten thousand from the market price. You see, in diamonds, the standard "30-day return warranty" does not apply. The best or the worst is to come immediately based on your opinion, and there is no "Sorry, I was wrong, I want to return the goods."

Upon closing a deal for rough or processed diamonds, a traditional phrase from the Hebrew language is typically used, the "Mazal and Bracha," which basically means "Good fortune and blessing." With this phrase and a handshake, the deal is closed, and there is no way to get your word back. He who changes his mind and retreats might as well consider himself omitted from the world of diamonds, i.e. the world of commercial trust because everything about this market is a matter of trust.

Back to our story, having found the Seckell family's soft spot, namely their shortage of cash, Karantoglou somehow helped them keep their access to the De Beers Sights, and this alone secured him a monthly income of 10% of the value of the rough diamond package. In addition, as Karantoglou had confided in me, the Seckells would also process the diamonds he was buying every now and then from Lesotho or from the black market using the Sheckells' connections, and, naturally, his own ones, which were increasing day by day.

Of course, I remember Mr. Pappas, from Cyprus, who was said to be going from cafe to cafe offering cheap, he claimed, unpolished diamonds. He was acquainted with individual prospectors (those looking for diamonds in their own estates or other public areas for which they pay rent) who preferred sales in cash unregistered in their books and, therefore, tax free. He gradually reached very high status without anyone knowing his sources (rumour had it that they stretched as far as Angola and Zaire). Everyone knew that he always had the largest number of rough diamonds, leastways those of great value. It was also said that he always travelled on his private jet. After fifteen years in this business, where his finest art was his range of acquaintances in the dark circles of blood diamonds, he had become a master. It was a fact that Pappas was a name inscribed in the notepads of every notable African prospector.

In the trade of rough diamonds, cash is the leading payment method. Some, however, had found alternatives. I had met an incredible Israeli dealer and diamond cutter who occasionally supplied me with polished diamonds, usually 0.30 to 0.50 carats. He used to tell me the plan he had come up with for buying rough diamonds from some Angolan villages not far from the capital. These villages had no electricity, hence, no means of temperature control, so the guy was providing the inhabitants with wooden ice coolers and the necessary ice brought in trucks, and he was being paid exclusively in diamonds. I had asked him back then, "Well, aren't these ventures dangerous?"

And he replied, "Yes, but I'm trying to make up for the school fees I've recently paid in Zaire."

And he started explaining to me that until two years ago, he had had a "good job" in Zaire.

"You know, the natives over there used to bring me rough diamonds from really far away and sometimes they had to cross the jungle. After a year or so of travelling around Zaire in my four-wheel SUV, they said to me, 'You know, boss, we have started being afraid to go back and forth on foot, because we might get killed. So, next time you come, bring all the money you can, and if you don't mind, we'll go up there in your 4x4 to purchase all the stock our friends have and get this over with for a while.' So I gathered all the money I had, borrowed some more from friends – of course in US dollars – and the next day, I was in Zaire, heading towards the jungle with three of my suppliers. After roughly five hours of driving, we reached a small clearing with some huts scattered here and there. There were no telephones, or any of your wireless means of communication back then, other than the sounds produced by the throat, so my friends started making jackal sounds. Soon, four men arrived, who began exchanging information with my own guys. I understood a little, such as how much money, what quantity. After I eventually took the money out of a hidden space I had made under the boot door, two more men came who made me count the dollars and told me that it was okay. The next moment, the guy behind me put a machete on my neck, and the other one asked me where I was hiding my gun. The result: they took all of my money and my gun. They also beat me on the neck with the back of the machete and left me lying half-dead in the middle of nowhere. Do you understand my current venture now? I am trying to at least make the money back that I had borrowed.'

Gruesome, yet original school fees.

But let's not forget Jonas Savimbi, the Angolan National Union for Total Independence

(UNITA) leader for more than twenty-five years, who had long been the primary pain of Angola's authorities and, in many cases, controlled the areas where the mines were located. It was said that most of the time, he pushed the diamonds to Belgium and often South Africa, where he could trade them for the weapons UNITA needed. In other words, it was not hard for the big players to find rough diamonds in the open market.

To become one of the buyers of such packages, you had to have a lot of cash or be a gun dealer. One such buyer was Karantoglou, who had the money and joined with the Seckells, who evaluated the packages and bought them if the asking price suited them. I verified this many times with Trevor, who, together with Moshe, used to go there to purchase big stones for their Japanese clients. They remotely knew Karantoglou, and Trevor used to say, "This guy must be loaded!"

During one of our evening meetings, Karantoglou described his dealings at the hotel in Lesotho.

He told me, "I usually sit in the hotel lounge, enjoy my Chivas whiskey and wait for the Seckells to first evaluate what is good and what is not. Then I take a look at the diamonds myself before giving them the money."

Chapter 6

Life went on. Dinos was running around in an olive-coloured Mercedes 280S he had bought to impress his new American girlfriend. This car was infamous because it had starred in a scandal that I will outline later. I've talked about a lot, but I haven't said anything about Dinos, who was, after all, my lucky charm because I had sold him my first valuable diamond and because he had helped me stay in business.

Dinos was a good, quiet boy, the kind you'd call "low-key." He had graduated from the so-called Minor Polytechnic University in Greece, something he rarely failed to remind us of. In fact, he used to carry in the back seat of his car one of those helmets engineers wear on the construction sites. When I realised it, I thought, *Well, if you want to make sure that a car belongs to Dinos, look for a helmet in the back seat.*

I went to see him in the new office he had opened next to the arcade on Commissioner Street, very close to Harrison Street in Johannesburg. After the usual greetings, compliments, and congratulations on his new car, we started talking seriously.

"I saw you the other day as you were coming out from Karantoglou's. You know that after selling the laundry, I've been working with him a lot because I need plenty of stones for my Afrikaner clients, especially in Pretoria," I told him.

"I know," he replied, "because I also procure most of my stock from Karantoglou, and in fact, we have made a draft of checks: I give him several checks in advance, and he pays me back with his own. This way, I can always have stones without caring to rush over there to sign, worried that I might not get exactly what I need."

"I believe you've given around \$250,000 in checks?" I asked.

"Yes, $290,000, to be precise, a total of six checks written every fifteen days."

Therefore, I thought to myself, with $450,000 I have reached by now, I am making a much larger turnover than Dinos.

"Moreover," Dinos continued, "Petros Bosikas – you may have heard about him, he is older than us – as far as I know, he does business with Karantoglou. And Panos Kotrotsios too, you know, the Greek-Egyptian who partners with Konidiatis, the one with the beautiful wife, who always shows up with the girls from Olympic air... He's a bit flashy— *no kidding!* Anyway, I've heard that Karantoglou is waiting for his family's leasing company to be upgraded to a commercial bank. Do you understand what this means for a diamond dealer? I expect him to buy the Seckell factory, and then I will probably take over sales management."

"Well done, Dinos. I think you will be able to hire your girlfriend too. Is it true she's from Florida? I saw her with you, I think the day before yesterday, as she was getting in your car.

Kudos, Dinos! Not because you are doing very well, but because I really like this woman. And your car, of course, especially the olive colour. The same as the one the Minister of Labour had bought and turned into a scandal. Really, wasn't it a Mercedes 280S?"

Dinos did not take the bait with my teasing comments, so I proceeded with more serious questions.

"Tell me about the Afrikaners, the De Jaggers; you're still working with them, aren't you?"

"Of course. I work very well with them because I serve many customers around the airport on their behalf. Suffice to say that sometimes I have to give stones from Karantoglou because the De Jaggers don't always have two and three carats available."

"Karantoglou told me that the Seckell factory works almost exclusively for him."

"Yes, I know."

Dinos paused for a moment, and then as if suddenly remembering something, he turned over and said to me, "Who cares! I'm thinking about my car, which everyone's talking about. We only live once. Look, I am a bachelor, and I need some kind of, how do you call it... bait."

"Of course, I know... I have seen the bird, a stunning woman. I heard she is imported. American, isn't she? Nice! Well done, Dinos, that's the spirit. What do you need the blinking money for? I wish you all the best!"

And I left, realising that I was not Karantoglou's only "good boy." The difference between Dinos and I was that I had a family, I had changed almost three different professions, and, of course, I had acquired some property, a fantastic house which, while not located in the "northern suburbs," had everything I wanted: a three-thousand square metre plot, an amazing garden with an Olympic-sized pool, six bedrooms, four bathrooms, an office... And I'm saying "northern suburbs" because in my discussions with my Jewish friends I learned that newcomers from Israel always asked two questions. The first was "which job makes the most money?"; the second, "which is the best neighbourhood to buy a house." There are many answers to the first question, but only one to the second, the one given throughout the ages by those of prestigious repute: *The northern suburbs!* And this applies in many cities around the world.

Conclusively, my visit to Dinos was good and constructive, not only because I liked him and wanted to see him but also because it gave me news about Greek people I hadn't met yet, our industry, and particularly our relations with Karantoglou. As far as I knew, many wealthy Greeks in Pretoria, especially Greeks from Egypt or Asia Minor, had placed money in Karantoglou's bank due to the strong relationship between the two communities and, as everybody knew, the family originated there, the outskirts of Smyrna, I think.

The market was a bit rough on the following day because the Black people of South Africa had risen again and were demonstrating. You see, the Afrikaner apartheid regime had been ruling since 1948 and had arranged it so that they'd get 80% of the vote in every election. This way, they did not bother much at elections and still maintained superiority, while everyone else – regardless of their colour or origin – were inferior, and non-whites were born to serve them. The mistake was that they firmly believed in this notion because it was being preached to them every Sunday in church.

Karantoglou called the same afternoon to invite me to his house for the usual, namely for drinks and discussions about work, the economy, and the general situation in the country and abroad. We started with the domestic situation – nothing new, but each new uprising was more severe than the previous one. Karantoglou was aware of my relationship with a local member of the government, Mr. Barend Du Plessis, so he usually expected more trustworthy news from me than that which is read and discussed by most people.

I met Barend Du Plessis during his visits to Tivoli, once or twice to buy cigarettes and another time for a book (you see, I was crazy about books, and I was always boasting all the latest notable editions). He had bought *A Theory of Justice* (John Rawls, 1971); I still remember this book. I had read it twice. Unaware of the client's profession, I had asked him if he was a lawyer because I had many lawyers and judges as customers since the city courts were very close.

"No," he had replied with a laugh, "I'm Barend Du Plessis, a member of Parliament."

This was the beginning of my acquaintance with the local congressman. (It should be noted here that the congressman's job in South Africa was to point out local issues in his region and forward them to the Parliament. From then on, he could not grant any special favours to anyone, nor did he have any Greek-like "liabilities" to pay). Our friendship was one between gentlemen, which allowed us to talk openly and freely about politics and general problems. In fact, he used to ask me about the issues of the Greek community. Of course, when I spoke to some significant and refined Greek families who agreed to invite Mr. Du Plessis for tea, in order to address these problems and listen to the relevant views of the government, some "wise" guys replied, "Why should I come, has he given me anything? Then why should I come to thank him?" That's all I have to say about Barend Du Plessis.

That night, Karantoglou seemed somewhat numb. I assumed that having the management of a bank on him, and in view of the current financial and political events, he had to monitor everything.

"You know, Frank," he said, 'for things to work smoothly and without problems, you must always be alert and in consultation with your major partners. I mean insurance companies, big banks, etc. That's why I have to make a trip to Switzerland tomorrow, to make arrangements with my bank there. I am flying tomorrow at noon, but I will be in the office at seven in the morning. If you want, you can come over, using the door I told you about the other day, to get some stones that you might need because I will be away for two or three days.'

The following morning I was there at seven sharp. As I was parking in the corner, Karantoglou was getting out of his car. It was as if we had an appointment! He waited for me, and together we took the stairs up to his office. "One minute," he told me as he removed a massive forty-five calibre, long-barrel Colt from the back of his belt. He said that he wore it there because it was so large that he couldn't put it anywhere else. I didn't comment on the fact that this weapon should better be kept in the office or at home than carried. He opened the safe and removed the cartridges with the diamonds, and after he wrote the Appro list I put them in my pocket and wished him a safe trip. As I was getting up, he stopped me, saying:

"Wait a minute, I have a check for you to deposit in your account; we keep forgetting it. You should remind me from time to time."

And he laughed. It was the monthly check of fifty-thousand dollars to pay off the one I had given him.

Having a lot of spare time, after I left I thought I'd pay a visit to Dave for some coffee and the latest market news. I found him standing and discussing with Trevor in an intense voice. They were talking about an acquaintance of theirs.

"Who's the one you are talking about," I asked.

"That fucking idiot, Israel Baruch, the pawn-broker with the minivan who goes around houses buying old jewellery and more..."

"What happened to him?"

And I learned the story. Baruch had an office near Carlton Mall, which served both as a place to receive customers and as a base for his ventures. A couple of days ago, in the afternoon, an unknown customer called him from Durban, claiming he was an Italian named Zitto Giacomo, a mechanic on a merchant ship coming in from Angola. Giacomo said he would be staying in Durban for three or four days and asked if he could visit him on the following day because he had something that might interest him. When Baruch asked him how he had found his name, he replied that another friend, some Van der Merve, a sailor on the ship, had made the recommendation. The next day, Giacomo came back with a small metal briefcase filled with bars of gold.

"Do you care for this?" he asked Baruch.

"I am always interested in good deals, but on two conditions," he replied. "First, I must examine the metal and second, check the gold content. If these are acceptable, I can give you 30% off on the closing price of the day."

The Italian replied that he would not take anything less than 22% off, always in cash. Baruch finally accepted the 22%, provided he would first examine the metal.

"By all means," he answered. "Take two or three blocks, examine them, and tell me when to come back."

At the same time, he emptied the whole briefcase, and after they counted a total of twenty-two bars, one kilo each, he put them all back except for two, locked the suitcase, and said, "Put the suitcase in your safe, and I will be back in two hours, either to close the deal or to collect my stuff and leave. I trust you because at least two of my acquaintances have vouched for you. Do you know Van der Merve and Koos Van Heerden from Umhlanga Sands? They spoke very highly of you and told me how much good business you have done together."

After the agreement was made, Baruch went to his Uncle Schwartz, known in the market as a fence for stolen stuff. The uncle told him, "You are lucky, don't even tell the president." After making the calculation, twenty-two kilos by roughly 25,000 rands per kilo equals 550,000 rands, minus 22%, he would have to pay 429,000 rands if he didn't manage to reduce the price a bit more.

He had one hundred thousand of his own cash on him, his uncle had another hundred thousand, and he called two more "investors", promising them quick profits. Investors of this kind were usually Jewish or Greek retirees, and housewives who kept their money under their pillow in 10x100 bundles, waiting for opportunities like this, instead of putting it in the bank. Other such opportunists could be prospectors or smugglers of rough diamonds or anything of the sort. Well, the necessary amount was always raised because the person of interest would start making calls to "listed members" who had enrolled to participate in such "opportunities". In half an hour, the money would be raised, and the deal would be closed. The clip holding the bundle would often be found rusty, signifying that it had been resting under the mattress for a very long time.

Israel returned with the money and waited for Giacomo. When he arrived on time, he told him, "Giacomo, I'm very sorry. I would like to close this deal, but I haven't been able to gather more than 340,000 rands. Apparently, our agreement is invalid unless you can accept this amount. You never know, maybe we can do something better on your next trip," he added knowingly at the end.

"What can I tell you except that you are lucky because I have to go. In fact, a guy from the ship's crew has come to pick me up in his rental car, and I will leave with him in an hour."

"I believe next time I will be better prepared because, you know, I have a lot of connections."

"I am not counting the money because, at this point, I believe in honour among thieves."

And this was the last he ever saw or heard from Giacomo, or whatever his real name was. The next thing he did was tell his uncle the good news about the extra profit of 89,000 rands. He then took the suitcase and immediately called his "specialist". It took the latter a while to examine the bars, and once he was ready, he threw the bomb: Of the twenty-two bars, seven were genuine, while the other fifteen were double-gilded copper.

"Stupid Baruch, you lost 235,000 rands only to make the famous Giacomo richer. If you were new on the street, I would have said, 'Okay, it happens,' but to be stepped on by an Italian with pretty words... Pay up," concluded Dave.

"Dave," I replied, "this is clearly what we call School fees. But in this case, we are not talking about school fees you pay off and forget, but about debts under your name, and there is no way to escape and continue living on this earth if you do not clear them."

These were the day's news, which would be discussed for many weeks in our circle – a reminder for the young to be wary of the many kinds of Giacomos.

Chapter 7

For many in South Africa, Monday is Blue Monday, while it is "babalas" for others. To South Africans, this is a well-known word meaning hangover after a heavy night of drinking. In fact, the locals would often use it in court to justify violations of all kinds. For me, Monday was a new beginning, a new page in business, and I always found myself trying to find "new fish to catch", as we used to say back on the islands.

That particular Monday, I was extra happy because, after forty-five months, I had received the prestigious diploma of Gemology from the GIA, which was – and still is – the highest degree in the gem industry. In practice, it is like comparing a practical healer, who might sometimes find the target, to a qualified doctor who is always on track with the specific line of medical science. Of course, the diploma alone does not make you a good gemologist. You must also have the chances and the luck to work with many stones and particularly with diamonds. I'm saying diamonds because at least they have been studied in detail, and there is a formula to price them according to established rules. Because I think it's immoral, if not criminal, to price a diamond beyond its value according to its position in the 4Cs. Knowing the rules, today I see many individuals owning jewellery that costs, in fact, nothing more than the value of the metal and the stones, who have paid a lot of money to buy them. If they need to sell it, they usually say that they are offered "peanuts" because they do not know that "peanuts" is not the money they are offered but the jewellery's actual value, which had been marked up by the seller.

I remember a relative in Athens who asked me to escort her to a jewellery store because she wanted to buy a cross pendant for a child's christening. We went to the store, the lady picked out two pieces and asked, "How much is this?"

"Thirty-thousand drachmas."

"And this?"

"Seventy-five thousand."

"Why is there such a price difference?"

"You see, madam, this one has a *brilliánt*."

"What is a *brilliánt*?" I joined in the discussion. "Do you mean diamond?"

"No, diamonds are another thing."

"Listen," I told him. "The *brilliánt* is a Greek invention for overpricing. They are nothing but diamonds, just very small, one to two percent of a carat, and because they are round, they are called brilliant-cut in English. You call them 'brilliant' but in a French accent. Give me a break! A 0.02-carat diamond, at 120,000 drachmas per carat, costs 2,400; make it three thousand to include the work. How do you charge 75,000 drachmas? Unless you don't know the difference between a melon and a watermelon.'

That's crazy stuff.

Once, my best friend's wife caught us talking

about jewellery, so she brought her jewellery box and asked, "What do you think of these, Frank?"

"They are beautiful," I replied.

"I know they're beautiful, but how much do you think their value is?"

"You're putting me in a difficult position, my dear, because if you ever want to sell them, you will think you've been ripped off and offered 'peanuts.' Peanuts are what you were given when you bought this jewellery."

To put it in a nutshell, we shouldn't always blame the pawnbrokers. Let's assume that the value of gold today is 652 rands an ounce, roughly twenty-one rands a gram of pure gold. The price of 18 carats is at 75%, i.e. 15.75 rands, while the price of 9 carats at 37.5%, i.e. 7.87 rands, and so on. A solitaire ring is usually crafted from four to five grams of 18-carat gold, worth around eighty rands. Including taxes, waste, and profit, let's say it is sold to the retail customer for three hundred rands. Now, let's go to a pawnbroker fifteen years later and assume that the market price of gold is now two thousand rands an ounce, that is 64.3 rands per gram, 48.2 rands for a gram of 18 carats.

The five grams of our ring are now worth two hundred and forty-one rands. Take out 5% for waste, it leaves two hundred and thirty rands, minus tax and profit, it would pay one hundred and sixty-one rands. Estimating that the price of gold is threefold its value when the ring was purchased, then our yield would be 67% of the metal's value. Not bad, I would say, because under no circumstances should we expect to get our money back. This is particularly true for the Greeks because they don't buy jewellery, but fashion and a bag with the famous jeweller brand to flash on their arm.

A relative once asked me if I had any diamonds on offer.

"Yes," I replied, "I have an incredible one, 0.81ct at four thousand rands, which is 160,000 drachmas."

"You have got to be kidding, Frank. Should I pay 160,000 for the stone when the ring costs 400,000? Are diamonds that expensive?"

Go figure it out with such an "education."

That same afternoon, I made my way to Trevor's factory. He was alone this time, and he started telling me about a former secretary of his, who had recently turned up again and would probably want to meet him.

"Why not," I told him. "You are still strong and attractive. What are you waiting for?"

"You know, I have arranged with her to come over here tomorrow afternoon after business hours, so I need you. When I return home late tomorrow, if my wife asks where I was, I will say, 'Fucking Frank came, he took me to the club, and we got drunk.' "

"Whatever, no problem, my friend."

I wanted to tell him about my diploma because, among other reasons, I wanted to make him realise that he would not be able to fool me when selling me diamonds. But, then again, I could tell him the next day while hearing the chronicle of his erotic adventures. I was flattered by his amiable manner and his trust in me.

I had to meet Louis that night because he had told me that he had money and a check to give me from the sale of a four-carat stone. He would also need a good one-carat worth around five thousand dollars for a new customer who was an old acquaintance. Fortunately, both Trevor and Karantoglou, before leaving for Switzerland, had given me some of these.

Chapter 8

The Greeks say that a good day starts with a good morning. I didn't believe much in this, because even the weather had changed lately. What had started with sunshine and clear skies suddenly changed into thunder, the clouds hiding the heavens as if the lord of the universe was sending all his rage over to you.

I was sitting in my office in Boksburg, going through my papers to decide my next move, when the phone rang, and Louis replied to my greeting.

"Frank, I will not be able to bring you the money, the seventeen thousand dollars I mean, because something has come up. Nothing terrible; I will explain to you later when I come to see you. What time in the afternoon? Are you going to be in the office at four?"

"I will be waiting," I replied and hung up.

The second phone call of the day came from Kaas van De Berg, Louis's friend and colleague. Kaas van De Berg was a skinny, forty-five-year-old guy, the type that is good at everything. An electrician by profession, he preferred working the odd job because he liked to chat. He had several acquaintances coming over, some were old contacts he had from his electrician job. That's why he was liaising with Louis as sort of an assistant. Until the year before, he used to work as an electrician in South Africa's only emerald mine, somewhere in the East of Transvaal. He didn't enjoy working there, so – can you imagine this? – he cut off one of his fingers to get insurance compensation. One hundred thousand rands, mind you, that was a lot of money at the time. The next day Kaas was driving a Mercedes, the dream car of many. Apart from that, he wasn't too bad a person, at least from what I saw initially. He'd usually come to my office along with Louis, or I'd meet him at

Louis's house in Pretoria, so I considered him as sort of an agent or apprentice. The first time Louis introduced him to me, he explained that he had a good family, he lived somewhere near the Cullinan mine, and his wife was a Public Prosecutor in the Pretoria Court. It was Kaas, who told me when I answered the phone, "You know, Frank, I know a wealthy guy who owns a real estate development company just outside Pretoria, and he was telling me the other day that he was seeking to buy a big diamond for his wife. I know he doesn't want any Afrikaner dealer, so if you want, we can go to his house together one morning, talk to him, and maybe you can make a small cut for me if all goes well. I will be happy with five percent."

That's the odd job I was telling you about.

At around four o'clock in the afternoon, Louis came by, smirking as if he had discovered something. I should note here that, following my advice, he had bought a microscope from the GIA three months before to show his customers the diamonds he was selling. Because most of them were located far inland, he always carried the microscope in his car. As soon as he sat down, he took an envelope out of his pocket, one of those envelopes used in the diamond trade. As he opened the envelope facing me, I saw a marquise cut diamond, yellowish but large.

"What's the size?" I asked.

"16 carats."

"Yes, but I can see some imperfections here."

"Indeed, it is low clarity."

"What's the story here, Louis?"

"It didn't fall off the truck, if that's what you're thinking, although you could say... yeah... you don't know Eric. He works downtown as a diamond cutter for the Wessel Brothers' factory. This diamond was 38 carats, and he bought it from a prospector in Western Transvaal. With his bosses' permission, he polished it in his spare time and offered it to me for thirteen thousand rands. Quite a bargain, I think."

"The price is reasonable, Louis, but who's going to buy it? The only good thing about it is its size. For jewellery, you can only put it on a necklace. If you have any old lady inland in mind, then good luck! From what I understand, my money has gone to buying this diamond, and what you're implying is that the faster you or we sell it, the faster I will get my money back."

"Well, something like that."

"Well, we might just make it. You know, I also wanted to inform you about a phone call I received from Kaas..."

And I told him about the proposal he had made me because, since Kaas was his client and partner, the right thing to do was to get his permission or at least inform him.

"Maybe this is just the customer we are looking for to buy this diamond. I know this friend of his ... let me remember... his name is Jan Prinsloo, yes."

"I presume Kaas doesn't know about this stone?"

"No, no, nobody knows about it at the moment. Prinsloo is rich, a bit of a poser, and he might be our guy because his wife, assuming he's buying it for her, will probably be thrilled."

"Do you think he might have a hard-to-get girlfriend, and he wants to bring her around?"

"I wouldn't rule that out. If we don't try, we won't find out."

"Well, let's do it," I replied after some thought. "How much do you expect to make?"

"Do you think two thousand is a lot?"

"I will keep it in mind as a reference because Kaas must also get a share if Prinsloo finally buys it. Leave it with me. Keep in mind that Karantoglou is coming back in three days, and we must definitely pay the pair of 1.15 carats each that we sold to Lombard."

As soon as Louis left, I called Kaas and asked him if his friend could see us the following day, because I had some stones for him. Kaas replied that he would call back in a moment and hung up. Next thing, I called Dinos first and then Dave to secure a few more large stones besides Louis's boulder, just in case.

The appointment was arranged. I had to meet Kaas in the morning somewhere on the highway outside Pretoria north, and from there on, I would follow his car to the prospective buyer's place. As we approached our destination, I noticed once more the large houses, their ten to twenty-acre plots enabling the owner to create his residence according to his personal taste. A while later, we entered an imposing property - around forty acres, I reckoned - with an equally majestic building. With the triple garage, the swimming pool with the pool-house around it, the barbeque and the bar on the side, it reminded me of the TV show "Dallas," an impressive copy of JR's house.

Something else that caught my eye was a caravan outside the garage. I thought I knew it from somewhere, I couldn't be wrong... and then, I remembered: Two weeks ago I had taken my Jaguar for service in the workshop of Frans Joubert, a former house engineer of Jaguar. Two caravans were parked outside the garage, one of them identical to Prinsloo's. I had asked Frans then, "Do you repair caravans too?"

"No, the one is mine, and the other belongs to a friend who sometimes leaves it here, in case we need to use them in the evening."

"What do you mean 'use them in the evening?' Do you go hunting or fishing?"

"Something like that," he replied with a laugh. "Many evenings we go out to parties or bars with friends who invite other people too. We take our caravans and park them at the corners of the streets where the guests can't see them. When everyone is wasted, some married women want a breath of fresh air, and... you understand, we offer immediate assistance as, by the time their husbands realise they're missing, they will have gotten their 'air' and returned. The trick, dear Frank, works very well, but we do provide social care since we offer immediate assistance to those in need."

After this finding, the feeling of "clean air full of oxygen" had stuck with me until we parked our cars in front of JR's, who was just coming out of the main entrance to calm the two Alsatian dogs and welcome us. It was already eight o'clock in the morning, and the sun had begun to rise. We entered the house, and, following the introductions, he led us to a living room overlooking the pool and a lush garden with stone tables and chairs all around them, and he asked us what we would like to drink. I imagined this place filled with guests for the traditional braai (the local term for barbecue). The host would have one or two lambs searing on the coals, and everyone would be drinking brandy, Coca-Cola, or beer - not so much wine – and eventually whiskey with Canada Dry ginger ale.

Prinsloo quickly dove into the topic saying that it had been a year he had been trying to find an exceptional diamond because he wanted to impress his wife on her next birthday, which was two months away. We sat in a cubicle in the corner of the room, with the light behind us, and I started talking about diamonds while showing him what I had, except for the big one. When I saw that he was not impressed with what he had seen, it was do or die time.

"I do have one, but I don't want to sell it. Not even Kaas knows about it. I got it for an American client who comes once a year for a safari in Zimbabwe. This year, he has asked me for a yellowish, big diamond, an outstanding one. He told me in confidence, 'You have to find something like that because if I don't go back with something outstanding for my wife, she will divorce me. You know, she's onto me messing around with my friends. You know, girls..." I explained.

"Do you have this diamond on you?"

"Yes. I didn't get the chance to put it in the safe this morning because it was still dark when I left to meet Kaas and come to you. You are forcing me to show it to you... So, here is a remarkable diamond, even more so because it has this colour, light cape, that's how we call it in the language of diamonds."

"How big is it?"

"Sixteen carats. Not such a common size, you must admit."

Once I opened the envelope, I saw his eyes open wide. Apparently, he had never seen such a big stone.

"Here it is," I told him, "cut perfectly for a necklace."

"Well, if we agree on the price, I will not let this stone get out of my hands, and I will also need you to design the pendant. You're right. The American will grab it right away."

I turned to Kaas.

"Kaas, will you kindly leave us for a moment? I want to tell our friend not just the price but how to make the payment too. You see, the owner of the diamond is a private individual, and he has the upper hand."

"No problem," replied Kaas.

As soon as he left, I turned to Prinsloo:

"I asked Kaas to leave because I do not want customers to answer to third parties for their spending or anything else. You see, many times, people talk for no reason about others' secrets. Now, without saying anything else, twenty-six thousand rands including the necklace: A simple, 18-carat gold, forty-five-centimetre chain with an oval-shaped binding tipped with one diamond 0.06 to 0.10 of a carat."

He squeezed my hands and said, "Okay, Frank, I am glad, even obliged because you preferred me over the American. Right now, I have fifteen thousand rands on me. I will give you the rest when you bring me the jewellery."

"It's a deal. And because I don't want Kaas to feel undervalued, you will give me fifteen

thousand now, without counting it in front of
him. He's a good guy but a little frivolous sometimes."

It was a good deal for all of us, especially me,
because I would otherwise have to squeeze Louis's debt, the seventeen thousand rands.

Chapter 9

The day was blue Monday, but it was a holiday, I can't remember which one exactly, one of South Africa's national holidays. This gave me time to go through my paperwork in the office to see whether I owed money, to whom and how much. I also took the chance to clean up my place; that is to say, I counted the official stock in addition to the cover stock. The latter is a stock of low-quality diamonds – we call them rubbish in the dealers' language – varying in sizes and colours. These are kept for import duties and the special tax, the Ad Valorem and Excise Duty – another bright idea of the government, which taxed the rough diamonds mined in South Africa as imported products, reaching as high as 35%! What did this mean for the diamond dealers? To buy in bulk from factories or other wholesalers, they had to have a registered AVED number and pay an additional 35% in advance. This money was only returned if the goods were exported.

All diamond dealers found a way to evade this tax. Once you have an AVED number, purchases and sales in your books should balance, at least weight-wise. Therefore, when you bought a total of 200 carats, you would try to get an invoice for a "packet of 200 carats, worth x amount of money" without details on the quality and individual sizes. It goes without saying that you wouldn't buy with your AVED number every day, but two to three times in six months at the most. Of course, the factories also tried to keep their books balanced accordingly.

When you had a visit by the tax inspectors, you had to hand over the keys to your safe for them to examine its contents and show the corresponding record in your books. I remember one day at the office of a fellow dealer in Johannesburg when the doorbell rang and we saw one of the tax inspectors in the security monitor. We dropped to the floor behind the door and lay there waiting, waiting for a long time, while the doorbell kept ringing and the knocks on the door kept hammering. When the man realised that there was no answer, he assumed that nobody was in the office and left, and we continued our work.

Naturally, it was not long before the solution was found (today we would call it a dummy start-up): Exports, many exports of polished diamonds. I had heard that a company based in Gaborone, Botswana was selling export invoices from South Africa, which means it was a company that imported "millions of carats of diamonds." The cost of each invoice ranged between 5-10% on the final amount.

Anyway, I tried to keep the books and the diamonds in compliance because you never knew. You see, I was not big enough to buy invoices from Gaborone.

My work effort was interrupted by a couple of young people who entered the reception of my office, so I got up, approached and greeted them, and asked how I could help. They were interested in a diamond suitable for a solitaire engagement ring. I started with the usual relevant questions:

"I know that women always have the first and foremost say on the diamond and the ring's design, but from what I see, the spirit among you is democratic; in a few words, you have decided what you want together."

"As a matter of fact…yes. We want to see a diamond for around seven to nine hundred rands."

"I see…"

I opened the box and placed three diamonds in a row on the diffuser plate, where you can clearly see the colour, the size, and the vibrancy of the gem. The way they looked at the stones, one at a time, and the way they chatted softly, made me like them. They were both around twenty-two or twenty-three years old, two sweet faces looking forward to the completion of their union. Finally, after hearing the prices – seven hundred, eight hundred thirty and nine hundred and fifty rand – they chose the most expensive stone, weighing 0.65 carats, which was precisely what they were asking for, and they would take it if we came to an agreement. When asked what deal they wanted, the young man confessed that they were University students due to graduate by the end of the year (it was still April).

"I work the night shift as a bus driver for City Hall," he said. "I can give you a deposit of one hundred rands today, and for the rest, I will be giving you as much as I can save each week until I have paid you off."

"You guys have really moved me with your manner and love, which seems sincere, and I totally agree with your proposal. When the time comes to make the ring, I will only charge you for the gold as a gift for your engagement."

After they had left, I was thinking of their situation and their joint decision for the engagement being the ultimate goal and not a showoff, as it happens with many couples, because I had seen many odd things during my tenure in the diamond business.

It seems like yesterday when a young man of Italian origin came to my office and asked to see a relatively large diamond, about seventy to ninety points of a carat, but below one thousand rands. After I showed him some options, he finally decided on a 0.92 carat at 920 rands, obviously low quality in terms of internal clarity, and he said, "I'm going to fetch my girl. You will show me all these stones again, and again I will decide on the same one. Do not mention the price. I will pay you when the girl leaves."

It was a great surprise when I saw one of the most beautiful women I had ever seen coming into the office. After playing our little charade, "this stone, no, that one," they finally chose the one we had agreed upon.

"Alright," the guy turned and said to the girl. "Go to the car, and I'm coming after I settle the finances with Frank." (He knew my name because he was a friend of a customer).

When the girl left, I asked him,

"Giuseppe, I don't understand. You have such a girl, the most beautiful girl I have seen lately, and you buy her this ridiculous diamond for an engagement ring?"

"Let me marry her first, and then I'll buy her

a bigger and more expensive one. What if she runs away? Should I lose the diamond too?"

Also, the couple that came one afternoon last week, around the time I was about to close. A guy entered dressed in the most expensive suit, the type you usually see people wear at the stock exchange, art events, fashion shows, or the theatre. The girl's outfit and appearance were similar, although her excessive make-up rendered a more "artistic" look. Anyway, she was beauty impersonated. Her body proportions – I would call them "balanced" – left no option to look at her face only and leave the rest out.

"I've heard about you," he told me in an unpretentious, friendly manner that you accept without thinking, *What is this guy talking about, as if we've known each other for a long time?*

He continued, "The idea is to find a diamond, not only for its beauty but also for its future value. I know it will cost a lot, but first, let's see what you can offer because, to be honest, we want to get engaged soon."

I started with two thousand rands.

'Isn't it nice, love? But how about a bigger one?'

This way, we went from one to the other to end up on a beautiful, yellowish stone of 2.5 carats, worth seven thousand three hundred rands.

"Yes, this is the one, love ..."

"Give me a kiss, my love," he said with a loving smile.

On the second kiss, the guy took out his checkbook and said, "Don't be scared; the check is for the deposit and not to buy the diamond tonight. We will come back tomorrow so we can choose the design of the ring as well. You know very well that design is always the girl's part, and in this case, Renee's."

He gave me a cash check for five-hundred rands, and they left, their bodies locked together in a sweet hug. The following day, shortly after I had opened the office, I received a call from the young man, Erasmus Keller, I presumed as that was the name on the check he had given me. He told me in a cheerful tone, "Perhaps you have already understood the spirit of yesterday's story. In any case, do not go to the bank to cash the check; there isn't a single penny in my account. You understand right? Anyway, I had an unforgettable night. What can I say, Frank, unforgettable! although I put in a lot of hard work. See you soon."

Chapter 10

It is incredible how fast the days pass, especially when you are overly busy. I was waiting for Louis and Kaas, who were both happy with the deal we had made for the marquise diamond.

Karantoglou had returned from Switzerland, but I hadn't met him yet, to find out what he had done and whether he had brought in more money to finance the business with our recently upgraded customer base. He called me at some point, and we agreed to meet later because, as he told me, something good had happened that made him change course, and he would need a lot of resources. And I understood.

A little later, I received a call from Niels de Wet, a hawker of sorts who rode the entire country down to the region of South-West Africa (today's Namibia), buying and selling whatever he came upon that could generate a profit. I used to call him "the Pawn Guru." He was an incredible guy who knew the country like no one else did, not by air or on a map, but road by road. He could start from the north and reach the south in his van, a one-tonne Toyota bakkie,[2] barely large enough to transfer the wares he bought from one place to sell to another. His repertoire covered everything, including, of course, old jewellery and stones. The other day he'd brought a fishing boat to Pretoria that he had exchanged for a small diamond, which Louis and I agreed to trade for another diamond. To list all of Niels's deals, I would need to write a whole separate chapter.

Anyway, he called me in the morning to tell me that "there were more fish than expected," and he would probably need my participation. He would try to meet me in person "because not everything can be said over the phone."

In those days, the collapse of the Kobus

---

2 Bakkie: South African term for the pick-up truck.

scheme was the headline in all the newspapers. This was a pyramid scheme that originated in South Africa in the 80s and later replayed in other countries including the United States. Adriana Nieuwoudt, the founder, claimed that his grandmother had found a plant that produced a thick, milky yeast culture that could be used as a skin product to produce miraculous results. Adriaan began selling dried plants that could produce 10 jars of culture per week. He sold these for 500 rands, and paid 100 rand per week to producers that sent him back a teaspoon of each jar's culture. He then resold that culture as an activator. Producers themselves would recruit new members to keep the scheme afloat. Adriaan, being the originator, quickly broke even, and the scheme spread, with thousands of people investing in this business, mostly from underdeveloped areas of the country. The South African government eventually declared the scheme illegal, but not before Adriaan pocketed a hefty $180 million. The ruling was that anyone that had benefitted from this scheme had to return their earnings, and Adriaan had to pay back all the money to claimants. Now, if anyone was to get their money back, that remained to be seen ...

I called Louis for news on this story for two reasons. If any of our sellers had lost or was currently losing money, we would have to be careful not to give them diamonds as we would be risking our funds. On the other hand, we had to keep our eyes open for new opportunities to sell diamonds.

At that moment, the doorbell rang, and Niels came in. He took off his backpack, put it in the corner, and sat down before saying anything.

"Care for a coke?" I asked him.

'You read my mind!"

His mouth opened with a smile, which I attributed to the satisfaction a customer feels when they enter the mini-market, and the shopkeeper asks, "The usual?" before handing them their favourite brand of cigarettes.

Niels was a man of medium height with rough features resulting from the life he led travelling cross-country in his bakkie. In South Africa, every man should have a bakkie - you are not a man's man if you don't have one. I also went around in my bakkie, not because of this reasoning, but because it solved the problem of parking in the city since you could park for free in loading areas (you should always carry a few empty or full boxes in the back). But even outside the city, it helped when you needed to load purchases for the garden or the house. Most of all, it didn't make you a target for thieves, as a diamond dealer always carries things of value. I remember my friends at the Rotary Club used to tease me, saying, "Frank has arrived in his bakkie full of diamonds. He has so many that he needs a truck to carry them." The fact is that Niels needed his bakkie more than anyone since he was always loading stuff, be that furniture, tools, light machinery, or whatever else came along.

I should note here that my bakkie came to me out of the blue. Last year, Niels had popped up once more on behalf of a farmer asking for a low-quality, 3.2 carat stone I had bought for around three thousand rands, while its market value was no less than five thousand. I gave it

to Niels for four-thousand eight-hundred rand
– an excellent price for Appro. In two days, he
called from the client's house, some four hundred kilometres away, to tell me that he could
sell the stone immediately, but part of the payment would be a VW Golf bakkie, almost new,
worth two thousand rands.

"*Mazal*," I replied. "Give it to him, bring me
the car, and I will pay you the difference of two
hundred rands."

We talked with Niels about various things. I
asked him if he had anything that might interest me besides diamonds – because he often had
old rings and other useful things I could sell or
barter.

"Let's come to the news of the day," Niels
said. "Do you still have the two big stones, the
5.80 and 5.45 carats, the yellowish ones?"

"Yes."

"And the other one, the 11.20 carats stone?"

"I can get it back once I talk to the owner."

I called Trevor straight away, asked him about
the stone, and explained that I would talk to

him later about the rest because my client was in front of me.

"Do you remember how much I want for the stone?" Trevor asked me.

"Yes, but since I cannot say the number, can you repeat it?"

"Twenty-one thousand rands. Cash."

"Perfect, I'll talk to you later. Oh, I also need a big favour. How soon can I have the stone in my office?"

"In thirty minutes."

"Okay, *baie dankie.*[3]"

I turned to Niels.

"Now, can you tell me what all this rush is about? What's the matter with you this time?"

"This time is a great time! I think you have heard about the Kobus scheme and Nieuwoudt's involvement. Do you remember when you sold the 3.2 carats and got the bakkie? The lady who bought the diamond is his aunt, so I have met him a few times. In fact, I helped him occasionally in his business. You know the bastard I am. When the scheme started to collapse, knowing

---

3 Baie dankie: Thank you in Afrikaans.

I was dealing with diamonds, Nieuwoudt called me and gave me an order to gather all the big diamonds I could find and transfer them to his headquarters, where he has two rooms full of money, lots of money. He told me, 'If I'm there, it's okay. If not, I have given instructions to the guards to let you in so that you leave the diamonds, take the money and go.' That's what I call trust. So, if you're in, take whatever diamond you can grab quickly, and let's go swap them for money!"

"My friend, you know me very well. I can live day and night looking for customers to sell diamonds, but personally, I cannot do such a thing, no matter how much money lies in front of me. So, let's talk about the present. There is trust between us, right? You'll leave me all the money you are carrying on you right now, I will give you these stones, for starters, and you go take a shot. Maybe the cultivation money will buy you more trips to exchange diamonds."

The doorbell rang just in time, and Trevor's delivery man entered with the stone. After he left, I said to Niels, "So, Niels, we're counting.

The money you gave me now is 12,500 rands. I am giving you three stones with a total value of fifty-five thousand rands. Your new balance is 42,500 rands. Here is the Appro book; write down the details and go for the catch, because I suppose you will not be the only salesman. Good luck to both of us."

Chapter 11

It had already been three days since his return from Switzerland, yet Karantoglou was nowhere to be found. He had told me he had to go to Lesotho to buy rough diamonds. He always went there with the Seckells, the father and the son, whose purchases he claimed that he funded. He would buy whatever he found in front of him, as long as it was a sizable diamond. Last year he had purchased a huge 62-carat reject. When I asked him where he planned to sell it, he replied:

"Dear Frank, this stone is waiting for the right time to be sold. I already have a potential buyer paying cash, and I could sell it to him for as much as threefold the cost of buying."

"Okay, you know more about the market, not

only in length, like me, but also in depth, which seems bottomless."

I made a call to Dave. I hadn't seen him for a while since our success with the "milk cultivators," as we called them, who had given us some remarkable profit at the eleventh hour. He was alone too, although Moshe had arrived the previous night for his monthly visit to Lesotho, where all the diamond smugglers drank their coffee in the main lounge of the only hotel. Dave always held information about all sorts of crazy things, so I baited him.

"If I find a rough reject stone, 60 to 70 carats, or if I hear that someone might have a stone like this, do you have anyone in mind as a potential buyer?"

"I will keep it in mind, although something strikes my memory..."

"One more thing. I want to repeat my advice to you. It is not a proposal because you make proposals for something you are involved in. It is a piece of advice, a benevolent attempt by someone who wants what's best for you."

"Come on, Frank, spit it out, although I can guess what the "advice" is on."

"Well, yes, I'm repeating it. I'm sure that you already have it in mind and that you have been contemplating it since the first time I talked to you. Trevor is great, and I think he loves you in the sense that he considers you an important, trustworthy, and good partner. Maybe he needs you more as an independent dealer than as his salesman."

"Thank you, Frank, but as I always say, I'm still afraid to go into my own business after that bastard cut off my wings."

"You'll have to do it sooner or later. The sooner, the better. You mustn't forget your uncle in New York, the one you have told me about so many times. I'm sure he will be one of your best customers."

'Okay, okay. The truth is that I sometimes think about it, and I have to admit that the idea almost excites me. You're right. I will have personal freedom and a profit margin since I will be able to work as much as I want and have as much stock as I need at my disposal, all on my own terms. I could look for a nice small place, two rooms plus reception, close to the centre... Thank you very much anyway, you are a good friend, and our cooperation will always be solid and honest. Mazal to you."

It is nice and good when you can help a person who had the misfortune of losing not only his money but also his momentum, even his self-confidence and his very faith in life. I often wonder why some people, while they have a lot of money and own businesses that create more of it every day, their minds are set on how to grab whatever they can hold in their hands from honest, hard-working people.

We all know that money is vital, but it is not the ultimate goal in life. "We need money, Athenians, and without money, nothing can be done that ought to be done," to quote Demosthenes. And Plato had said, "Wars are occasioned by the love of money." I personally agree with Mark Manson and his quote, "Money is merely an arbitrary store of value. It is not value itself." I believe that money is not the source of wealth in human life; it is the result. People often assume that money is the cause of their problems, while in reality, it is the consequence, perhaps the most noticeable one. Friends and relatives often kill each other for pecuniary differences, usually insignificant. Of course, given that one's basic needs require a reasonable amount of money, one can and must save for a rainy day.

Once, at a Greek social gathering, I met Mr. Vogiatzoglou, an accountant from Smyrna, who had studied in Athens and held a master's degree from England. He asked me if I had time to stop by his office to see some precious stones in his possession. I remember him opening his heavy-duty safe and pulling out a boxful of various jewels, including an 18-carat rough emerald and two or three diamonds. Then he took out a 33-carat rough emerald. We talked a lot about the economy, the situation in the country, and other interesting things. He was a pleasant type who liked today's dates but didn't fail to see a little further into the future.

So I asked him, "I don't think it's just your love of gemstones that has turned you into a collector because, between you and me, your collection is worth a few hundred thousand dollars."

"You're right," he replied. "I read a book once that said, 'it is better to light a candle than to curse the darkness.' Wise people take precautions, but insightful and prudent people have the advantage. This may seem weird to you, if not cheap philosophy, but it is the fulfilment of my mother's wish to me.

I was born in Smyrna, and I was in the second grade at the time of the massacre. My family – father, mother, sister – and I were lucky because we managed to embark on one of the first ships and arrived alive in Greece and finally in Athens. I will not go into details, but I will tell you one thing: had my mother not managed to smuggle two rings and a necklace with expensive precious stones, we would not have made it. Selling the rings, we survived for a couple of months until my father, a specialist in the textile industry, found a job. Ever since then, my mother has been saying, 'Kids, remember this adventure we've been through and the role my jewels have played.'

So Frank, no matter what you own in real estate or in the bank, a situation may come that leaves you with no control over these assets; there is no need to convince you of this truth. Look at Egypt, for instance."

At that moment, I remembered an Egyptian pharmacy student I had met during my college years, who was renting an entire apartment on Thiseos street in Kallithea and had invited me to his birthday party. He had asked me to go there beforehand because he couldn't decide which suit to wear for the occasion. When he opened his wardrobe, I understood why: there were a dozen of them hanging there! However, when his parents got blockaded in Egypt – In the end, they couldn't even board a plane with their jewellery because these were snatched during passport control – he had to give up his apartment and sell half of his clothes for peanuts.

My reminiscing was interrupted by Mr. Vogiatzoglou's voice.

"... not to mention Kenya, Tanganyika, Zaire, the Congo. I believe that Hellenism has been persecuted in the last century. I think that, with

these words, you have understood my own ap-
peal for jewellery and stones with real value.
Of course, one cannot invest in precious stones
and jewellery without some sufficient knowledge on the subject. I have met people with lots
of money who spend their lives trying to find
new methods to deceive others for pennies."

We had a similar conversation with Karantoglou the other day, and we laughed. I had told
him then:

"Just think, Dem, could you see yourself doing something like that!"

Chapter 12

The money or the box!

Once a factory has finished polishing a batch of rough diamonds, they calculate their total cost and usually put them in a special leather box. If there is a buyer for the whole package, then a really facetious bargain begins, "the money or the box", which I personally enjoy very much since I always buy at a fair price.

Because of this, that afternoon I found myself in a relatively small factory owned by Johann Grobler, an old friend, who had a box ready containing the diamonds of the last four days.

"What's in the box?" I asked somewhat mockingly.

He gave me a list, saying, "I'm giving you ten minutes to decide what you want; specific stones or the whole box."

I wrote down "$15,000" on a piece of paper, put it in the box, closed it, and passed it over to him.

"Your turn now, I told him. Let's start with how much you want for the box, and then we will see."

"How about eighteen thousand four hundred dollars?"

"No, you are far off."

"Sixteen hundred. Rock bottom."

"No, you are still far away."

"Well, open your cards then."

"My cards are inside the box. I'm going to the toilet. Take a look, and we'll talk when I come back."

When I returned, Johan glowered at me.

"You fucking cunt, you want to screw me again."

"Why, my friend? I, too, have to make a living."

"Okay, give me $ 15,450, and the box is yours."

Of course, I left with the box, which I "broke

down" immediately upon returning to my office. The diamond dealer is always wary of the merchandise in such cases because the estimation of the total and the purchase are made really quickly. However, this is the only way to buy at a price really close to the cost of production, with a reasonable profit for the factory. Sometimes you can even buy at cost or even further below since the factory can always make a mistake when estimating or cutting the rough diamond. Calculating the difference between the box's average wholesale price and the purchase value, there was a 25% gain for me and a reasonable profit for the factory because rarely can one sell all these stones individually. And don't forget their need for cash, necessary for subsequent purchases. While the dealer, under normal circumstances, does not have to keep his own stock. All good.

A phone call from my insurance agent interrupted me. He wanted to thank me for the check he had received that covered all the insurance policies I had with him: the house, three cars, and the Jeweller's Block Insurance Policy

I had made three months ago. Awesome safety for diamond dealers and jewellers! Once you had signed the contract, you had full coverage against theft, robbery, loss on your premises, or even on the street. The downside? The premiums you had to pay per month since the insurance company was Lloyds of London. Only an organisation of this magnitude could hold such insurance terms.

It is a big advantage to have an insurance broker, a lawyer, good auditors, and, as I later realised, one, or better yet, two police detectives on your side. You would think that I have overlooked one banker, but I disagree. While bankers are essential for supermarkets and other businesses, they're not as indispensable for a diamond dealer who can have the money he wants by selling diamonds to others, as long as his name is worthy.

All you need from a bank is the manager to occasionally confirm if the funds in a customer's account are sufficient to cover the check he has given you. A lawyer is necessary to get you out of complicated legal situations or out of prison if it ever comes to that.

David Du Plessis was new as a diamond dealer, not very clever, somewhat slow in thinking, but a good all-around man. I met him at the Kaplan Jr. factory. This small unit usually procured rough stones from Sightholders who broke down their Sight box and retailed the rocks individually or in custom batches. From time to time, when they had a difficult stone to process, they'd call David's father to help because he was one of the best diamond cutters, even though he was retired. From that day on, David would come to my office to discuss diamond issues and get my opinion on handling several situations. Soon after that, he shared with me his adventure, which eventually turned out to be another case of a "student" who paid his school fees very dearly.

After graduating from high school, he was immediately thrown into the diamond business with the help of his father. The latter still worked in the factory of Barry Jankelowitz, a businessman and diamond manufacturer. He started selling diamonds for Jankelowitz, got acquainted with other dealers and began to make money. Nevertheless, as he told me, he didn't even change his car, a Volkswagen Beetle, which he still drove.

Back then, in South Africa, people of Indian origin (a community of more than one and a half million) mainly worked with textiles, flowers, jewellery, and many of them as travel agents. Mr. Aurel was a well-known goldsmith of Indian origin, located near Meyerton, about fifty-five miles from Johannesburg. He quickly became David's best customer as he needed stones, usually small but often large too, for the jewellery he made. Things were going smoothly, Aurel mostly paid in cash upon receiving the stones from Dave, and everything worked like a Swiss watch. But it seems that even the best watches come to a point where they fail to show the time correctly. Aurel started to ask for more stones at some point, paying half in cash upon delivery and the rest by "next week." An experienced dealer would have understood that something was wrong, but not David.

A year or so had passed since the beginning of the David-Aurel relationship, with good times in selling. David's father was a skilled cutter, but craftsmen are usually good at their craft while not as good at trading. You see, there is something unique about diamonds: They are small in size but large in value, so trust between the two ends of the transaction, the seller and the recipient, is imperative. A dealer should start feeling afraid if suddenly a good customer claims he has "customers who have come from overseas and want a lot of goods".

Well, in our case, Aurel said he had foreign clients from Canada and had to gather a considerable number of diamonds in different sizes and value. There was a chance, he said, they would even ask for stones worth hundreds of thousands of rands, so David, being Aurel's main diamond supplier, had to do his homework. He picked twenty-three stones worth 150,000 rands wholesale and 180,000 retail. Good profit for a day's work. Things, however, did not come as expected because Aurel simply had other things in mind. *He* was the one who left for Canada or wherever else he had planned to go. Of course, he had taken David's stones, along with jewellery, pound sterling, and expensive watches from other merchants because when one is preparing such a trip, he should make it worth the trouble. In short, David's school fees cost him only 150,000 rands. 78,000 out of these, namely his and his father's stake, were immediately erased, but he was still liable for another seventy-two thousand for stones he had taken on Appro. He was now driving a Beetle not because he still liked this car, but because he didn't have money to buy a new one.

The good thing about him was his honesty to declare his situation before politely asking:

"Frank, if you can, from time to time, give me some stones to sell. You know my situation and that I'm not a petty crook."

"Okay, David, the limit I'll set for you is four thousand rands. Try not to spoil it," I replied after giving it some thought.

Chapter 13

I could hardly remember what day it was that morning, an insignificant detail to me since my time was so full and my activities so many that I was only focusing on my present and future endeavours. However, I did remember that I was expecting a new client to come by, Jan Campbell, who had called from Vanderbijlpark, south of Johannesburg.

At around eleven, he was in my office. Young, tall, a bit sloppy with a fashionable dealer's purse, he struck me as somewhat preoccupied. He took out a neat solitaire ring without a stone and asked me to measure the size of the rock he would need to nail because he was also a diamond setter. I measured some 4.3 millimetres, which roughly meant a diamond of 0.35 carats. He took his time looking at various stones before finally deciding on one worth four-hundred rands. He packed his ring and said, "I'm going to get the money from the car. Hold the stone. I'll be back in four minutes."

Four minutes had become twenty-four minutes when I took the envelope with the stone to put it back in the box. Something was wrong; I could not feel the rock's volume at all. When I opened it, it was empty. I ran out on the street towards where I thought he'd left his car, but of course, he was not there. At that time, a hard punch in the face would feel nothing compared to the slap given to me by that hotshot, Jan the nailer! I looked everywhere, up and down, back and forth. My friend, the stone was gone, and so was my reputation as a guy with foresight in the diamond business. I had lost my virginity not to a professional thief but to a small-time thug. On the plus side, at least the loss was not so terrible in value.

I immediately called my insurance broker, who started laughing and said, "There is a first time for everything, my boy."

I submitted my claim, and pretty soon, the Inspector from the Lloyds of London visited me to find out how my loss had occurred. No problem. They shortly sent me a check for four hundred rands, and as expected, next month, the premiums had gone up 20%.

While we're on the subject, I remember two incidents related to a popular scam that some Jewish associates made occasionally and at least six-seven months between scams. One morning, when I visited my friend Dave's office, I found him talking to Slom, a diamond dealer originating from Iran. I knew Slom used to pass by his office, carrying a small bag where he kept his diamonds and his invoice book. He was supposedly selling diamonds, but when asked to show his goods and the prices, he presented the invoice book.

"Take a look here; I give all this at cost."

"And what is the cost?"

"What you see in the book. I sell at cost, only because I need some money."

Whatever diamonds he had were listed in his

book at the price he wanted to sell, which he called "cost price." Anyway, Dave was telling him:

"Well, Slom, you can have five hundred rands straight after your return, which will take less than an hour on foot... Yes... you will come to the corner of Bree and Rissik Street, on the Rissik Street side. I will be approaching Bree at that time. You will walk towards me, I will fall down and yell, 'Help, they're attacking me.' You will grab my purse, run to my office and wait. Neil will come from the adjacent street (Neil was a neighbour Dave used for his scams), running down and shouting: 'Thief! Thief! They hit a diamond dealer! Have you seen anyone running?' Leave that to me."

He turned to me.

"If anyone asks you, you will say that you were in my office an hour before the incident, and you saw the stones I had in the box, particularly one of 3.25 carats, G colour and VS2 clarity."

"I see. I will be a witness to the contents of your box."

"Yes, that's the idea."

It's simple and, with a bit of luck, easy to implement, as long as nobody passed by to witness the setup. You've probably figured it out already: Based on his insurance policy, he claimed compensation for the whole box. The money he received was enough to cover the premiums for the previous as well as the subsequent six months.

Nor can I forget Leonard the Big Boy, one of the richest diamond dealers in Johannesburg, with connections in New York. I used to buy the occasional stone from him, especially when I was in Johannesburg, always after noon, around two to three o'clock. This was the best time to buy from Leonard because he would be returning a bit tipsy from his lunch break with his secretary, a beauty not older than twenty-five years. That was the only time Leonard could make a mistake in estimating a diamond and an excellent time to buy from him.

One day in Dave's office, Leonard came along

and greeted us with the smile of a fisherman who had just caught a huge salmon.

"How are you today, Leonard?"

"I'm great. Here's why."

He opened a small bag and took out one of the most beautiful diamonds I have seen: 5.25 carats, D colour, VS1 clarity, almost perfect. I reckon the selling price would be around forty thousand rands per carat.

"This beauty is for sale," he told us. "If either of you has anyone interested, let me know because I will have the stone for 48 hours, and then I will send it to New York."

Later on, when I went to my craftsman, Harry, to collect a ring I had ordered, I found Leonard with his beautiful stone once more. The same story again. In fact, Harry told me, "Leonard will take the stone and show it to every dealer in town. But this is crazy. Unless...'"

"Unless what?"

The next day was a mess; insurance brokers and the police were asking one after the other dealer if they knew about the stone Leonard was trying to sell because when he got in his car to go home the previous night, the stone had disappeared.

By the way, Leonard had an all-inclusive Jeweller's Block Insurance Policy...

Chapter 14

Karantoglou was the one who had sent me to Harry, the goldsmith, to have my jewellery made. From what Harry was saying, Karantoglou gave him a lot of work, mostly engagement rings and necklaces, as well as various bracelets; you see he had his sister working for him and running everywhere. His sister was a few years younger than Dem, but she was what you call sharp as a tack. She was always running around, and I had seen her hooking well-known wealthy Greeks, and of course, making their jewellery.

As I approached Harry's workshop, I saw Dinos coming out, with whom I talked on the phone almost every day. He told me he was delighted with his new office, which was in an excellent commercial location. He had done a marvellous job, with nice furniture and a powerful microscope imported from the US. He also worked almost exclusively with Karantoglou, besides some Afrikaners with whom he had worked with for a long time.

In the evening, I passed by Karantoglou for our standard whiskey session. After the usual small talk, he started telling me, "Well, Frank, I'm in discussions with another factory to take over sales of their production, our strength is growing. You know, I'm going to make Dinos the sales manager at the Seckell factory. And when I say our strength, I mean the ease of finding the goods my customers want, my heavy artillery: Louis, Snyman, Niels..."

"Good for you, Dem, I'm delighted. Now I have to leave you because I have to go to the bank, you know, Standard Bank in East Rand, to sign a Broker's Contract with the Johannesburg Stock Exchange for Krugerrand[4] gold coins."

---

4 Krugerrands: South Africa used to be the world's leading producer of gold. In 1967, the government introduced these gold coins weighing one ounce as a legitimate way for private individuals to buy gold.

What did this mean? I had started to sell Krugerrand and Sovereign gold coins. If a customer was looking for gold coins, with a phone call to my broker at the stock exchange, I closed the price and, upon agreement with the customer, I placed the order, which usually arrived at my office after two or three working days. The payment was made from my bank account (enter the crucial role of the bank manager, who would act as a guarantor, a prerequisite for becoming a broker-dealer for gold coins). In addition to personal recognition, I also had a 3% brokerage commission, not great but enough for future customer service in diamonds.

That night I had invited the said bank manager to my house for dinner, to show off my culinary skills. You see, cooking was and still is a personal pastime for me because, in addition to the satisfaction of creating, it also offers absolute relaxation.

There was a fishmonger in the Bruma Lake Mall supermarket, with fish as good as the guys

---

The success was so big, that by 1980, Krugerrands covered 90% of the world's gold coin market.

serving and cleaning it. The young men behind the counter were from Mozambique and knew everything about their job. With a small tip and a smile, you could make those kids feel great. I had given them my phone number to call me whenever they had a good catch. So, last night they called to tell me that they had three cape salmon, roughly two and a half kilos per piece. I ordered all three of them, and in two hours, they were on the grill. My friend, the manager, was lucky to have fresh cape salmon that night. He deserved it because he was good to me, honest, and quite friendly.

The following night, I was at Karantoglou's house again, and when I told him about my new brokerage business, he replied with a laugh, "Frank, I think I have made you the best customer of the bank. Just consider how many checks from fifty to one hundred thousand rands you hand to this branch. This is amazing, not only for you but also for the branch manager, since you have increased his turnover. The other thing I admire about you, Frank, is that you have discovered excellent Afrikaner dealers, with so many connections to wealthy farmers."

"As for Afrikaner dealers, bless Louis, Dem. I've told you a bit about him, he's an accountant, and that was his first job until he discovered that his clients, some second-grade diamond dealers, were making three times the money he made."

"Yes, I know, he eventually turned to diamond dealing. Especially after he met you and managed, with your help and knowledge, to "unlock" a number of great connections and move forward in this business. I also know that he always seeks your opinion as guidance when making a decision. It's an incredible accomplishment if you think about it!"

"You know, his interest in geoscience has landed him another side job and parallel 'sport.' He has become a prospector of precious stones and metals. All these accomplishments give him a special place among other Afrikaner dealers and businessmen, and yes, my presence has been a tremendous help to enhance his image as a capable dealer.

Every Saturday morning, Louis and I attend

the big auction in Mabopane, East of Pretoria, you know, the one where everything goes under the hammer. Louis has connections there through his driver, and he auctions our jewellery, stones, and whatever else we can sell. As a matter of fact, we even auctioned a fishing boat once. In the afternoon, we went to downtown Pretoria, where another auction was held by a good friend of Louis's. You have been to my house several times, so you must have noticed the latest TV models and even a Vespa near the bbq grill. Well, these I've gotten at auctions.

Talking about bbq grills, and before I forget: On Sunday you are all invited to my house for a braai, your parents too of course. You know, last time they came, they made quite an impression on my religious mother-in-law. For days she was saying, "What nice people they were! As soon as they entered the house, they rushed to kiss the Virgin Mary in the icon corner, bowing and crossing themselves." If you want any particular appetisers with ouzo, like grilled octopus, let me know.

"What are you saying, my friend? Your appetisers are as unique as your kindness is. We will be there as usual, at around twelve-thirty. It is a good time, I think."

When I arrived home, my wife had news.

"The farmer who had bought the diamond from Dinos called you. I remember. That was the first diamond you ever sold, and it made such a difference because it had raised your morale. Do you recall?"

"How can I forget...?"

Nicolas Lombard remembered me. Here's a good omen. Of course, I returned the call immediately. After the usual chit-chat, Mr. Lombard cut to the chase.

"You know, I still have an appetite for diamonds."

"That's good news, not only for you but for your wife too," I teased.

"This is true, because she, too, has participated in the farm and bean cultivation. And since we have sold our production, we have decided to invest in a diamond or diamonds. The money is in the kitchen drawer. If we give you around fifteen to twenty thousand dollars now, what do you think you can secure for us?"

"I will look and get back to you tomorrow morning."

In anticipation of the upcoming sale and the potential profit from "the beans' cultivation," that night, I was brimming with excitement which I successfully channelled into the marital bed. Later, at around two in the morning, my wife and I set off for a fantastic trip to the East.

By dawn, we had already covered five hundred and twenty kilometres. The sun rose slowly to give life to the herds of oxen and cows that were starting their breakfast with green grass. On the other side, you could see mountain slopes covered with cultivated forests financed by German paper companies, as I was informed.

As we approached the house, a vast complex with a swimming pool, a guest house, and an open space for braai, we found Nicolas and his wife waiting at the gate to lead us to the garage and from there to their enormous kitchen, where they had prepared breakfast. We left

two hours later, lighter by three carats (two diamonds, 1.5 carats each) and richer by ten thousand dollars. I consider this one of my greatest
professional successes, as Nicolas was essentially my first return customer.

Chapter 15

I buy with knowledge, and I sell with integrity. This has always been my motto and principle for any business or activity, and life in general. Especially in the diamond business, extensive knowledge builds your reputation as an expert, which in turn brings loyal customers. Buying with knowledge is a challenging yet one-and-only road for a good professional. The people you work with should also know because the capacity and expertise of one person cannot guarantee everything. Beyond knowledge, trust is even more critical, from the merchant to his dealers and suppliers, and vice versa. We all know many companies that suddenly went bankrupt, taking down their associates and

investors with them. Dropping like that is un-
questionably deadlier than one of your associates failing to come through.

According to the GIA, the prerequisites for a
good salesman are the following: First of all, he
must have confidence and trust in himself. This
quality is enhanced by knowledge. Second, he
must be incorruptible and honest. Third, and
most important, is knowledge, an indispensable
virtue in high-class sales.

The diamond is a unique material because
carbon forms crystalline systems of the highest
symmetry in nature, known as isometric or cu-
bic, which render their exceptional properties:
hardness (it is the hardest substance on earth),
a high degree of transparency, refractivity, and
dispersion. Polishing enhances all these properties to produce this fiery brilliance that makes
diamonds cherished above any other gemstone.

The more I read and learned about diamonds,
the more I felt overwhelmed and fascinated,
and the more I loved my profession.

I am saying all this not to impress you but
to show you my appreciation and admiration

for these stones and remind myself that I need to continue with my studies. Because, as the De Beers slogan states, *diamonds are forever.* This is true because while the diamond is one of many gemstones, it is the only one that has been extensively studied and classified, allowing for its accurate valuation throughout all stages, from rough to polished stone. It is imperative to know that the net price of the gemstone is the same all over the world, and what changes are the taxes and duties imposed in different countries.

Personally, never in my life have I tried to misrepresent or overcharge my trade, and I have always tried to keep an integrity balance: a reasonable profit for me, more profit for you. Everyone doing business with me knew my mentality, and above all, my main supplier, Karantoglou. What great satisfaction and confidence he should be feeling having a partner and friend who, in addition to being honest, also brought in more business.

My thoughts were interrupted by the ring of my phone. It was Dawie du Toit, a good customer who, together with his partner, Derek Walker, owned a small steel construction factory and bought diamonds every now and then. This time they wanted to purchase gold Krugerrands. In less than an hour, they were in my office, where they told me that because the price of gold had recently dropped, they were thinking of buying twelve pieces. After a short discussion with my broker, I informed the customers that the value of their order was 6,250 rands and that it would be delivered in two to three working days, namely, the following Tuesday. Typically, when a client orders a batch or even a single gold coin, they have to pay in advance, but I did them the courtesy of trusting to get paid upon delivery. Huge mistake!

On Tuesday afternoon, my customers arrived to collect the Krugerrands in my safe. They said they were very pleased, but they handed out 5,800 rands instead of 6,250. When I told them that they were wrong, they replied that the price of gold had further dropped, so they should pay the current price. Their theory was madness. Try as I might, it was impossible to change their minds even as I explained to them that the coins had been brokered at a specific price. There were two things I could do at that moment: Either keep the Krugerrands, something I didn't want because I would block six thousand rands, or sell them, which was also bad because it would make me look like a profiteer. I tried explaining to them again. It was a waste of time; they were not going to give up. I was in an awkward position because I did not want to disappoint them. I weighed it all in my head and finally told them to take the coins and that they owed me another four hundred and fifty rands. They took them and left.

That night, I played the incident over and over in my head until an idea came to me. I remembered that two weeks ago, they bought a 1.20-carat, light yellow diamond for five thousand rands. At the moment, I had another one, 1.50 carats, similar colour but lower clarity, at a price that covered the cost of the coins and left a profit for me. The following day I went to their factory.

"Listen, my friends," I told them. "I know

you are not happy with what happened with the Krugerrands. So, I thought I should make it up to you, even at my own expense. Give me the coins, and you will get this diamond without any extra charge."

I tell you, they were thrilled.

Chapter 16

I cannot remember what day or month it was... I do remember that it was around noon. I did not have much work to do that day, so I was cleaning my revolver, which I kept in my office safe lately, while I had a shotgun at home for safety. Earlier I had visited the bank to deposit some money along with a check from Karantoglou for thirty-five thousand rands. The weather was not the best that day. Many clouds had gathered around noon, making me think of the darkness well before the beginning of the night.

The phone call that came was from the bank manager. I wondered what was on his mind after the beautiful evening we had spent together at my house a few days ago, and I thought he might want to invite us out.

"How are you, Frank?"

"Not too bad, my friend. How are you, is everything all right?"

"Everything is fine... You know, Frank, we have a small or maybe a big problem. The check you deposited today, the thirty-five thousand rands by Mr. Karantoglou, has returned unpaid."

At that moment, had someone passed me this news and then said, "it was a joke", I would have laughed; I would have laughed hard. It can't be possible for Karantoglou's check to bounce, and for such an insignificant amount no less!

"Are you serious now?"

"Yes, I spoke to the manager of his bank. The truth is you have to see it in person, Frank. People and businesses do not remain forever the way we would like them to be."

At that moment, it felt like a bucket full of chilled water was poured over my head and down my spine. I was so stunned by the shock that I could hardly understand where I was and what had happened.

The next moment I called home to tell my wife that something had happened and that I had to go to Johannesburg immediately. I locked up at the office, ran to my old car, a Chrysler Charger, and headed to Karantoglou's bank in Johannesburg. Freaked out, I rushed into the manager's office.

"I apologise for barging into your office like this, but I need your help. My name is Frank Hasides, and I am a diamond dealer from Boksburg."

"Yes, sir... Frank, is it?"

"Yes, Frank from Boksburg, a diamond dealer. I need to find out what happened to a thirty-five thousand rand check issued by one of your clients, Mr. Karantoglou."

"Yes, Mr. Hasides, I have also spoken to the manager of your bank. I must caution you, and I am sorry to tell you to be worried if you have more checks pending from Mr. Karantoglou because the funds in his account are drying up... Try to stay away. I am telling you this because your bank manager has spoken very highly of you. Be extra cautious and try to distance yourself from Mr. Karantoglou's accounts; this is official!"

"But," I said, "what about his leasing company?"

"He is very clever, that Mr. Karantoglou. When he saw the tsunami coming, he transferred his shares to a limited liability company in Switzerland."

I left the bank and drove straight to Karantoglou's office, where I found him sitting with his tail between his legs. When I politely asked him what had happened and why his check had bounced, he replied nonchalantly:

"Don't worry, my friend, everything is under control."

And he turned to his father, who was also present:

"Let's find a big diamond and a few more to give to my friend Frank for now."

I was left in doubt. Because it was late, I first went to my office to ensure everything was in order and then returned home, where I told my wife everything, and we both decided to wait until the next day to see what would happen. Meanwhile, I called Karantoglou and asked him to return the rest of the checks I had given him for the next six or seven months, worth 440,000 rands. I got terrified for good when I considered his travels to Switzerland, about twenty-three in the last few months, and his cheap, as I now saw, stories about his private bank. Anyway, I said to myself, we will see what happens next.

As the end of the week approached, I had to check on my dealers in Pretoria. In my supply, I had a big diamond sold to Dinos's bosses by a Cypriot lady for cash, various stones from other suppliers, but very few from Karantoglou and mostly the cheap, "rubbish" stones. I had to return them to him as soon as possible because I was afraid that he was even capable of falsely charging them as valuable ones. The love and friendship I fostered for him had been broken forever. I was afraid. I stopped eating. I'm not sure if I had eaten anything in that whole week. My wife did everything she could to help me, telling me not to worry and that this was something minor, impermanent, a crazy story. I said the same and much more to myself, too: this could happen to anyone in our business and other theories to soothe my worries.

On the other hand, I wondered how such a large and powerful diamond dealer could have financial problems when his business seemed to be running smoothly, especially given that his turnover from my sales alone reached a few hundred thousand dollars per month. One thing was sure: From now on, I would no longer be the same person. I felt violated, that awful, suffocating feeling that I imagine other victims have felt. I called Dinos to find out if anything similar had happened to him.

"Yes," he replied. "I do have a similar check for fifteen thousand rands, which also bounced. I spoke to Dem, and he explained everything. He has paid two million dollars for a box of rough diamonds, which are currently at his affiliate factories for polishing, and he will soon have them on the market, so everything will be paid then. I'm not that worried, and I think neither should you. Dem is a clever old fox, I'm telling you."

"I hope you are right, Dinos."

Two or three days later, I returned the "rubbish" stones to Dem, who assured me that he would take my checks back from his bank safe. On the fourth day, the bucket that doused me was double, and the water was not chilled but frozen, turning my head upside down, wondering what exactly had happened and where it had come from. It was when I received a call from one of those offices that buy checks or promissory notes, usually at half price.

"Is this Mr. Hasides?"

"Yes, how can I help you?"

"'My name is Jeff Cardoso, and I'm sure you know why I'm calling you."

"No, I don't."

"I see. However, you do know Mr. Karantoglou, since you have been working together for a long time."

"Yes, but what's the meat of the issue?"

"The meat is that we have a number of your checks signed to Karantoglou, which we have bought for a total amount of 290,000 rands, starting next week. We are wondering whether you would be interested in buying them back as a lot at a much better price or if you would rather pay them on the expiration dates you have signed."

"Neither do I know you, nor have I signed any checks over to you."

"Of course, you have not signed any checks to me, but you did to Mr. Karantoglou, with whom you have been in business with for a long time."

"I will catch that thief first, and then we'll talk again because you sound like half a thief. I am not in a position to speak to you anymore," I said and hung up.

Almost immediately, the phone started ringing again. I thought it would be the same person and prepared to speak not politely, but in my dirty language. It was the voice of a lady asking if she could talk to Mr. Frank Hasides. Assuming it was a potential customer, I said:

"Yes, you're speaking with Frank."

"One minute, Mr. Frank, Mr. Andre Abraham wants to talk to you."

"Hello, Mr. Abraham, how can I help you?"

"Let's see, maybe you can help me. I am the General Manager of Money Solution, a private discount company. I must inform you that I have several checks signed by you for the total amount of one hundred and fifty thousand rands, starting the first of the following month. If you are interested in buying them, I will see what I can do for a good discount..."

Chapter 17

My life started before World War II, and until I was thirteen, I had known nothing but killing, guns, and war. However, what happened to me today was inconceivable. My best friend in the business, the wealthy, imaginative, successful businessman, with many dealers below him and a big factory working for him...my friend...the backstabber!Human senses just couldn't comprehend it.

My mind went back to the conversations we had once upon a time, particularly at that time when I told him, "Don't try to screw me..." and he laughed. He was probably thinking about this day, and thought that I would not be able to see it coming nor stop it from happening.

I was still his partner and "friend." We had not quarrelled, nor had I threatened him. Next, I touched my revolver, and my mind began to make plans. It was effortless to enter his office unnoticed through the back door, as he had shown me so many times. A single bullet would be enough, especially coming from his big Colt gun.

After I had finished dinner with my family, I apologised and left, telling them that I was going to look at the stock market performance and arrange payments in my office, although all I wanted was to concentrate on my plan. All plans were made in my mind. I was clever enough not to write them down on paper. I would start very early, not later than six in the morning, to allow enough time to get to Simmons Street and wait for him at the back entrance of his office, pretending I wanted to talk about the stock market. We would walk together up to his office, where he would open the door, turn off the alarm, and then, as usual, take his revolver off his back holster because, otherwise, he wouldn't be able to sit down. At that very moment, I would grab his pistol with my left hand, holding my own gun in my right, just in case he was fast. Either way, he would get shot, be that with my forty-fiver or his Colt. I preferred the second scenario because it would make it all look like a suicide, a reasonable assumption given the problems he was having. I had already arranged an appointment with Louis at ten in the morning, at his house in Pretoria, where I would arrive very quickly via the highway. I planned my rout. I would leave Boksburg heading towards Edenvale, and before reaching the motorway, I would turn to the eastern ring road of Johannesburg. From there, I would take the first exit, straight to my "friend's" back entrance to stop his "charitable" activity once and for all.

That morning the weather was cloudy, and anyone who had lived in the area long enough could tell from the smell that rain coming. All the better for me, because there was less traffic on the streets and, who knew, maybe a better day lay ahead. I started implementing my plan without breaking my usual daily routine so that nobody would notice anything different. My bakkie was in order; no one would look at it twice on the street. I was no longer in the habit of drinking coffee, so I left without making any noise that would wake my family. I had already told them about my morning appointment in Pretoria, so everything was fine. From a psychological perspective, I was overwhelmed with a feeling of independence - and superiority. You may think that I'm talking nonsense, but it's like I'm living it again right now. I did not feel that I would save the world, but merely myself and a few others with me too, because I was sure that many had been harmed like I had. All night, I was thinking that things could easily and quickly go wrong and that I hadn't calculated all the possible consequences. I stayed up thinking, and as the night progressed, the feeling of pressure increased, as if I had a mountain on my chest.

The rain started as I was driving towards Edenvale. Fortunately, I knew the way very well because I had driven that route many times; my mind was not clear at the time. I thought about the present and what I would do to get rid of my bad luck. I thought about the past. I remembered the house I was born in, nothing grand: a small bedroom, a kitchenette, and another adjoined space for dining and other family activities. The bedroom was for my father and mother, the floor of the family room was where the children slept and doorway led to the dining area that was used once or twice a year for family gatherings and holidays. On top of the dining buffet were two brass artillery shell casings used as flower vases. On the wall behind the vases, and above the buffet hung a framed embroidery with the sentence, "Destiny is unavoidable", expertly stitched in silk. For some reason, that I had no time to analyse, I couldn't get this sentence out of my mind.

It was pouring, and as I approached the freeway junction from the west, ready to join the south freeway to Simmons Street, a terrible thunderstorm started. The storm was slow-moving and I managed to leave it behind.

I saw that as a sign of good luck. There was a slight delay on the ring road exit to Simmons, which is not uncommon when entering the city via the highway. I had plenty of time, as I was only a hundred metres away from the office, seven minutes ahead of the estimated time. At that moment, I could not believe what I saw: Karantoglou was parking his car, an old grey Ford almost unsuitable for driving, which he drove because, as he said, he did not want to make car manufacturers rich. I felt like a cat approaching to grab a fat mouse. The difference was that I was not going to play with my mouse but rather send it to meet its Creator.

I was just about to go upstairs to his office when he saw me with the corner of his eye and turned around surprised.

"Hey, Frank, you've been on my mind all night long. I was hoping to meet you today. Come on, let's go upstairs."

Surprise? None for me. I couldn't forget the frame in my parent's house: "Destiny is unavoidable". Luck was on my side; everything would be straightforward. Even if I had been rehearsing this murder for weeks, things couldn't have gone that perfectly.

Karantoglou disabled the alarm, unlocked the door with his keys, and we went inside. As expected, he took the Colt out of his back holster to put it in the top drawer of his desk. At that moment, I don't know what happened, he stumbled and almost fell on the floor with his gun. This was my chance. I grabbed the gun with one hand, while with the other, I helped him stand up. A loud thunderbolt was tearing the sky as I lifted the Colt to hit him. He burst out laughing up to the moment he saw the barrel in front of him.

"Destiny is unavoidable."

As I was about to pull the trigger, a flash of reason hit me for a nanosecond: I saw myself in court and in prison for murdering my friend and colleague, and my family on the street... Oh my God, what was I about to do? This image struck me like lightning, and I felt it all the way down my spine. I burst out laughing, not normal laughter, but the nervous type, and we sat down until the storm had passed and silence had prevailed.

"Take your fucking gun," I told him, handing him the Colt. "I don't need much temptation to shoot you."

I said nothing else; I just sat in silence, waiting for his answer. The only thing he said was, "Don't worry, Frank, I will fix everything. Things don't always come the way we expect them to."

Chapter 18

I used Karantoglou's phone to call Louis in Pretoria and apologise to him for postponing our appointment; it was not all that necessary anyway. I went straight to my lawyer in Benoni, from there to my office in Boksburg, and then home. The feeling of freedom that overwhelmed me when I was about to kill Karantoglou had transformed into satisfaction similar to what you feel when winning the trophy in a challenging game or competition. I was the winner of the day! I had gained my life, my family's life, and our future, all in one big winning day. I would drink to that as soon as I got home.

On the next day, I went to see the bank manager - and my friend until yesterday - to see what he had to say. He had invited me to his office, not as a friend anymore, quite rightly so, since he didn't know the extent of my involvement in this story.

"Mr. Hasides" (not "my friend"), "I have asked around, I have also talked to the manager of his bank, and I'm sorry to tell you that you have been involved in an illegal scheme. We, the bankers, know it very well and call it 'kiting.' You are in a terrible "check kiting" situation, and the outcome of your problem is highly uncertain. I am telling you this because in the two years that I have known you, from the history of your transactions and the general opinion your customers and the public have on you, you seem like a hardworking person and a good family man. From what I hear, you also have good standing within the Greek community, where everyone says that you work toward its benefit. Personally, I believe that the man I have met and worked with in the past is principally worthy. In the name of our friendship and as a bank manager, I advise you to try to prove your innocence, start paying, if you can afford to, and take it step-by-step to the Court of Law."

I thanked the bank manager and friend of mine for his suggestions and kind words, but more so for the light he had lit, which would be the beacon on my way to making the dark sky shine bright again.

My next step was not with friends but with my opinion – which I had formed from the experiences of clients, friends, and acquaintances in the community who had suffered similar disasters. Above all, I had faith in my lawyer, Mr. Slomowitz from Benoni, and appreciated his advice. (I always remember this city, Benoni, because I associate it with Benigni, the famous Italian actor). Mr. Slomowitz was relatively young, around forty, but very smart and highly knowledgeable about the law and its fine details. He had represented me every time I needed a good lawyer, always with an excellent outcome.

I dropped by my house for a while to show that I was well, and to my great pleasure, no one understood my condition. Then, after my brief stop, I drove to Slomowitz's office, all the while thinking about nothing else but my story, how I would present it to him and his colleague, David Bearn, how quickly they would grasp my case and if they would understand my agony. I was talking to myself as I walked in, "I'm not crazy, but if I find an explanation, I cannot guarantee anything."

"Mr. Slomowitz, I am here to get an explanation and your legal advice on my adventure. According to my bank manager, I am involved in a financial scam, the infamous 'kiting,' all thanks to Mr. Dem Karantoglou."

Mr. Slomowitz asked me to follow him to his office. Once I stepped inside, he quickly started in his usual, straightforward manner:

"Frank, let's talk about your problem. Let me understand it, and please keep the explanation as brief as possible."

"You're aware that I deal in diamonds. My boss... if I can call Mr. Karantoglou that, because he is my main provider of diamonds. I either sell the diamonds and give him the money, or return the diamond I am not able to sell... I am sure you know how it works."

"Please continue, Frank,"

"Well, Mr. Karantoglou – his name is well known in the market – has played me. He has conned me out of almost half a million rands with a scheme the bank manager called 'kiting.' The whole issue began with me signing checks in good faith, but Mr. Karantoglou thought otherwise."

"You're crazy, my friend," he replied in the stern tone he usually kept for Court. "You should know, Frank, that Mr. Karantoglou's current worth is enough to buy the Johannesburg Stock Exchange. My brother is a lawyer, and has been consulting with Mr. Karantoglou regarding one of his companies, namely his new bank."

"That's bullshit, Mr. Slomowitz," I said, feeling overwhelmed with the stench not from the dirty money but from the shit that they were trying to feed me.

In response to my trash talk, he said, "Everything will be fine, but it's getting late now. I will call you early in the morning."

"Fine," I said and left.

As I was returning home, I realised the depth

and the extent of Karantoglou's grip on the money market. I congratulated myself for my courage to stop at the idea of killing the man who was my partner and supposed friend. As I was taking the last exit from the highway to Boksburg, I began to feel the warmth of my family, and I was looking forward to talking to my wife. I might even speak with a Cypriot neighbour, a nice guy who had come from Ethiopia, and with whom we had family gatherings every once in a while. The only sure thing at the time was that I wasn't going to pay for the stolen checks and that I had no intention of talking to Karantoglou about it. I could see clearly now that his frequent trips to Switzerland were not to meet with his partners, as he had claimed, but to move there with all the money and the diamonds he could grab.

I also called Dinos to find out what had happened to him. He was going crazy, from what I could make from his voice. He had lost some one hundred and fifty thousand rands in checks similar to my own story. Moreover, as he was close to other clients of Karantoglou's, he had learned that each of the dealers he worked with had lost a relatively large amount too. In his opinion, though, the worst case was the Jewish family of the Seckells, who would lose their factory because their licence would be suspended due to the financial scandal, and who knew how many others, as more and more people turned up.

After meeting and discussing the situation with my family, I decided to go under, in other words, to declare bankruptcy. The final decision would be made after discussing it further with my lawyer and after getting further legal advice. It seemed that I would not have a calm night of sleep from then on, so I decided to give similar peaceful nights to my friend Karantoglou. At two in the morning, I called his home line. I heard his voice saying, "Hello ... hello ... hello?" three or four times, and then, following my silence, the handset dropped. I would continue this for the rest of the month.

The next day I visited the Diamond Club, the most prestigious organisation for businesses and dealers in the trade. I was not a member yet, but I was going to talk to them anyway. The general manager was a well-known diamond dealer in Johannesburg, and he knew my good reputation. As I was telling him my story, I realised that he was already well informed by other members who were involved too. He thanked me and assured me that as of that moment, the Karantoglou name would be out of business. This meant that no dealer or jewellery store would be doing business with the Karantoglou family from then on.

In the afternoon, I went to my lawyers in Benoni after calling to make sure they would be there. Mr. Slomowitz was standing in front of his office and invited me straight in.

"Frank, I'm really sorry about yesterday and the opinion I expressed. You are one-hundred percent correct. Mr. Karantoglou turned out to be one of the biggest crooks my brother has ever met. As a matter of fact, he wants me to pass his thanks to you because had it not been for our conversation yesterday, he would probably find himself seriously involved; you see, everything happened so fast. I'll tell you one thing:

I congratulate you on going after him. If anything, the pending tsunami has stopped."

"Thank you," I said, "but let us put this aside,
for now, to talk about my situation and what I
should do."

"Alright. I have thought about it in detail.
There are three options. First, I can declare you
bankrupt. In this case, I must explain to you
that you will lose everything in your possession
that the law can touch, and of course, the brand
name and the ability to maintain or open a bank
account, and whatever comes after that. If this
does not seem like a good idea, the other way is
to pay or try to pay the companies that deposit
your checks, and on the way, we'll see how we
can take action to defend ourselves, but this is
a very long process. The third solution is to pay
them all off and then see what we can do."

"No way! I would never even consider giving a single penny to scums of this kind. I'm
sure that they knew what they were doing when
they paid the amount agreed with Karantoglou.
Anyway, I will tell you my plans by tomorrow,
and we'll continue. I assume Mr. Bearn, your

colleague, also believes and agrees with what we have discussed.'

At that moment, David Bearn came in to announce some new information.

"I know at least one company that has bought your checks; this is their job, to lend money and discount checks. I know the owner is a Cypriot lawyer who inherited a large sum of money from his father, an old man who for all his life owned a cafe near the centre of Johannesburg, above Simmons Street. The old man sold the premises and the cafe, which had been standing there since the city was formed, to a large British firm, and he died shortly afterwards. His son, soon to be our opponent, found himself with a lot of money, so he closed his law firm to take the easy way of making a profit by lending money and discounting checks and promissory notes. He has lost a lot of his father's money and will try to compensate with whatever he can get from us. In my opinion, he is a stupid guy who does nothing else but drive around in a 60s Porsche, one of the brand's first coupe models. We still have a few days until they deposit the first checks. In the meantime, you can think about it and, whatever you decide to do, we are here to help."

I returned to my office to check my books. Everything was in legal order. The stones I had in the safe corresponded more or less to the purchase and sale invoices. I quickly examined the qualities and values I had, and after that, I called my rubbish-diamond provider.

"I need some 25 carats of the rubbish you have for me, dear boy."

I visited him and bought the carats required to balance the weight in my books, put them in the safe, and removed everything else of value that was not listed in the books. I went home, and after explaining the situation to my wife and agreeing on everything, we went to the bank where I had my life insurance and signed it to be transferred to my wife so that there would be no life insurance under my name for them to withhold. I stopped another insurance for an-nuity payment, took all the cash I could gather and put an amount aside to cover my current liabilities to Trevor and De Jagger. The rest – I cannot tell you how much – I gave to my wife for the rainy days to come.

Early the following day, I went to Trevor.

"How much money do I owe you?" I asked him.

"What's with this attitude? I did not ask you to pay me."

"Yes, Trevor, my friend. I have to pay you today because tomorrow I may go bankrupt."

"Frank, you're an asshole. If you are going bankrupt, as you say, why are you paying me?"

"I want to pay you because I don't intend to go bankrupt to get money from you, but…" And I told him in detail what had happened to me.

"You know," Trevor replied, "I've always had my doubts about this bastard Karantoglou. Mr. Seckell had also told me some things… I will spread the news to other factories to keep him out forever."

"Anyway, you can get the nine thousand I owe you now, and we'll see what will be next."

"Thank you, Frank. Whatever you need from me, just let me know."

Next, I called the De Jagger factory and spoke

to the general manager, Mr. Groenewald. I told him what I had said to Trevor, explaining my situation to him, which he already knew, as he told me, from the Diamond Club. He sent over his cash collector, and I handed him the eleven thousand dollars. I was left with a plot of land I had bought when I started my business in South Africa for twelve thousand dollars in instalments. It included an old farmhouse, which I rented out to an old Afrikaner for eighty dollars per month. Because it was located next to an old farm road connecting Boksburg with Benoni, which the State had decided to expand. One-third of the plot had to be expropriated according to the official plans. About eight months prior, they sent me a letter to inform me of this decision, offer me twenty-five thousand dollars as compensation for the part they would take and to ask me if I agreed so they would send me the relevant check. The amount was more than good for me. The piece of the plot that I was left with was what I would lose if I went bankrupt. Let them have it! I was thankful I had been paid long before that day.

We had some new furniture in our house, and they probably had the right to get it. My Cypriot friend and neighbour came to the rescue. Since he lived close to me, at night we moved everything to his house to "rest". I gave the cash I had along with some stones to a friend from Zaire, who also lived nearby. I am not exposing their names for obvious reasons.

I also had to talk to my lawyers about the house, whose titles were under both names, mine and my wife's. David had the answer.

"I know there is a Greek custom where men ask for a dowry when they get married, something similar to the transfer of cattle to the bride's family that is customary in some African tribes. The difference is that the Greek men *receive* money from the bride's father. And without a doubt, I will claim that I am sure that the house is a present from your father-in-law for your marriage. According to the law, the State recognises it as an asset that cannot be appropriated. Presto! Problem solved, no one can touch your traditional gift."

I still had time to visit Johannesburg's top

lawyer, Mr. Abramowitz, who knew my lawyers and shared their opinion. He also knew the situation with Karantoglou, who had managed to con some Greek businessmen in Pretoria out of their money, besides his dealers. "The dice had rolled," as our cleaning lady used to say.

Next, I called my lawyer to ask what it would take to tie the knot in this case.

"You will bring a person to sign for your bankruptcy, he said. Do you have anyone... Not a relative, however?"

"Yes, my friend, and in fact, someone very close," I said, having George in my mind.

The following day I borrowed George from his wife and the Cafe he worked in, and we went to Benoni to sign that I had borrowed from him one hundred dollars in the last six months, and I never paid him back. That was enough to send me down to hell. Because going bankrupt to make money is one thing, while going bankrupt to punish someone is another.

Chapter 19

Bankruptcy is declared for two possible reasons. It will either be targeted, i.e. a person or a firm goes bankrupt with the sole purpose of conning associates and stakeholders out of money and assets, or it will be chosen as the only way to save someone from the teeth of financial predators who have deceitfully appropriated or targeted his belongings. My case fell under the second category for all the reasons dictated, plus one more: to send the kite-master to Court or to drag him down with me.

Immediately upon the declaration of bankruptcy, the Trustees, together with the creditors, take over. According to the law, a Trustee is appointed by the Court to manage the debtor's property to the benefit of the creditors (whoever these may be). His purpose is to prioritise the claims and make payments accordingly. Therefore, once you have declared bankruptcy, the Trustees come into your life for good and become your big boss. Your Trustee knows everything about your life and your career so far; he also knows and has a list of every asset under your name.

In my case, he came to my house, listed everything around, and then went to my office, where he got all the keys and automatically became the boss. In fact, he came with my Cypriot "creditor," the petty man I mentioned earlier, the one with the antique Porsche. The only thing I regret today, after everything, is that when they asked for the combination to the safe, I gave it to them, while I could claim that I didn't remember it or something similar. The safe was a small one, about seven hundred kilos, with a key and a code, nothing special, worth around five hundred dollars. It contained all the diamonds registered in the official invoices and all the relevant books. The furniture amounted to almost nothing, meaning that their total value was not more than five hundred dollars. There was nothing else under my name, apart, of course, from the rest of the plot.

ZEN, the Trustee firm, was probably the largest of its kind. I think I was lucky because besides being an excellent lawyer and accountant, my Trustee, Mr. van Niekerk, also had a lot of experience and understanding of the local community. I spent the first day discussing with him and answering his questions. From the beginning, I was impressed by the opinion and knowledge he seemed to have on Karantoglou and his family. The first thing he said after our nearly day-long contact was, 'I am truly sorry, Mr. Hasides. It is unfortunate to encounter such predators. Nevertheless, you should know that from now on, and until we have further information, I must have a list of your activities in terms of work, financial gains, etc., by the end of each coming month. I mean, total income, so much in rands, from such activities. Total expenditure, et cetera..'

In other words, he wanted a detailed record

of income and expenditure, always with the purpose of acting on behalf of the creditors whatever money was left.

My wife was into art and women's fashion and, ever since her first small shop with ballet accessories, she had always had her own business. So for a while, she would bring income to the family until I could get off the hook and go back to the trade I knew; diamonds. Fortunately, no one in our circle had in any way or by any means lost money because of me.

The first meeting between the creditors and debtors, the debtor in my case, was scheduled for the following Monday. The month was February, almost autumn. I had a feeling that something would happen and I was excited, not so much for that scammer Karantoglou, but mainly for the other swindlers, the Cypriot "financier" and the other one, the General Manager of the financing company which, as I had found out, was in Portuguese hands and mostly drained off Portuguese companies (which were generally similar to the Greek ones: small mini markets, grocery stores, fish shops and the such, hence, also sitting ducks for these cannibals). According to my Trustee, the first general assembly would be for our opponents to make the first contact.

"And you should know, Frank, that I say 'our' and not 'your opponents' because I have figured out everything about Karantoglou's set-up. The guy has driven out of business at least four major companies and one diamond factory, who had worked with him for a while, maybe a year. He had given them a few thousand in the beginning, to snatch a few million in the end. You have to remain calm, Frank, and we will see how the whole story goes. In addition, you must know that these people are, in fact, mobsters with their own police detectives at their disposal to investigate everything about you for hidden assets, diamonds, cash, or anything else of value."

I thought that the only thing they could do was pump me regarding the rubbish diamonds in my safe and perhaps try to change the legal certificates on the origin of my house coming from dowry. It was Friday, and it was easier to meet and talk with my lawyers because both of them were "battling" in Court during the working days. I found David, the one I was actually looking for, and discussed it with him. He was pleased with the words and the overall attitude of the Trustee, Mr. van Niekerk. He outlined his plan to take legal action against Karantoglou on the charge of Fraud in the First Degree. In this case, we would need witnesses, actual witnesses who had suffered, like my friend Dinos.

The meeting with the creditors was at five o'clock on Monday afternoon, but I arrived much earlier. My Trustee introduced me to his general manager, emphatically, if you ask me, and the manager greeted me in a somewhat apologetic manner. I don't know what's gotten into me, perhaps because I did not know what I would face, but for the first time, I "wore" my flat pistol in my belt, on the left-hand side, to easily pull it out with my right hand if needed. I was feeling so much hatred for these dogs that I was prepared for anything because no way would I buy that they were not in on the game with Karantoglou. I knew that if they tried to force me to do things that would be detrimental to my family's finances, I would revolt.

We started with the Cypriot, who appeared to have done his homework on diamonds:

"How come the diamonds we found in your store's safe were only low-quality?"

So I answered back, "What kind of diamonds did Karantoglou promise you, and on which principles did you buy my checks, if you have bought them at all and you are not playing games with me, claiming money for checks you have never bought? And how did you trust a scammer to buy checks before making sure they were sound and not bounced? Therefore, sir, stop asking questions because you will not get any answers, and keep in mind that I, too, will be checking your status in the market soon because a lot is being said by the people around you."

"Mr. Hasides, you should be a little more careful with your words."

At that moment, Mr. van Niekerk intervened to answer the initial question on the quality of the diamonds I had left behind.

"You should acknowledge, gentlemen, that Mr. Hasides' previous occupation was owner of a dry cleaner until Mr. Karantoglou recruited him into the diamond trade. Lacking specialised knowledge, he possessed low-quality diamonds, not because he chose them, but because Karantoglou convinced him to, and they were left in stock. As for his other assets, I have them all in my report, and I do not think there is room to offend an otherwise serious person like Mr. Hasides. His economic strength and honesty in his transactions are well-known to the Greek Community and the broader circles of the diamond and jewellery trade."

This way, the first contact with our creditors ended smoothly.

The same afternoon I was sitting in my home office planning my next moves when the phone rang, and an unknown voice replied to my greeting.

"My name is Frikkie de Jager, and I'm calling from Springs. Your friend Nicolas Leventis gave me your number, and I would like to meet you to talk about doing business."

I couldn't refuse, so I asked him when he could come over.

"You know, Mr. Hasides, I can only come after business hours, at around eight if it's okay with you."

So I arranged the first appointment with Frikkie, an acquaintance that was meant to go beyond business and evolve into a long relationship of close friendship and mutual appreciation.

Later that night, just as I was getting ready for bed, the phone rang again. It was my lawyer, Mr. Slomowitz. I wondered what he wanted; probably for me to go to his office in the morning to sign the lawsuit against Karantoglou.

"Frank," he started. "I wanted you to hear the news from me right away. We cannot go to court against Mr. Karantoglou and we don't need a lawsuit. My brother just informed me that Karantoglou was forced into bankruptcy - he is losing *everything*. I was so thrilled that I wanted to share the good news right away."

For the first time in weeks, I felt the refreshing breeze of clean air fill my lungs as relief washed over me. Then my words of warning to Dem Karantoglou came rushing back to me. "Don't try to screw me, because I will respond in such a way that you will not be able to tell the difference between your head and your ass."

Mr. Slomowitz continued, "Fear not. You going bankrupt has forced the two 'financiers' to go after Karantoglou to recover their losses. More than a dozen other people have also come forward with similar claims against Karantoglou. He had no choice but to file for bankruptcy. This is only the beginning, and you threw the first stone to *take down Goliath*. Well done, my friend!"

As the dark clouds dispersed, I hoped I would never see the man, nor hear the name "Karantoglou" ever again. But "destiny is unavoidable."

About the author

Alex Tsotros is a Gemologist (GIA, FGA, JCSA) with over 45 years of experience in the global market of diamonds and precious stones.

He has lived in Johannesburg, South Africa, for more than 30 years, where he worked as a diamond dealer and was granted a special license by the government to trade and process rough diamonds. Since 1980, he has been a partner and coordinator of the Gem Education Centre, a training institution accredited by the Jewellery Council of South Africa, offering diamond grading and accreditation courses (incl. GIA & FGA) to professionals from around the world.

He is a member of the World Diamond Council (WDC), the International Diamond Manufacturers Association (IDMA), and a Diamond exchange member with the World Federation of Diamond Bourses (WFDB), among other clubs and associations.

He currently lives in Greece, where he was born and obtained his first University Degree from the Agricultural School of Athens in 1962.

Dear reader, after you have read my book,
I would be very grateful if you visited my
book's webpage on Amazon and posted a
brief, honest review. Thank you!

Alex Tsotros